# THE
## Rich
### ONE

THE ESCORT SERIES VOLUME 1

# N.O. ONE

Cover design – Crowe Abbey Covers

Editing – Encompass Press Ltd

# WARNING /
# FOREWORD

**Before you continue**

The Rich One is the first volume of a series of six.

It is graphic and morally on the fence, containing extreme-ly sensitive material that may not be adapted to your needs.

If you need specific details of things involved, please visit our website for a list of warnings.

www.author-no-one.com

If you're okay with all of this, just remember... we warned you.

On the plus side, the lead female is strong and proud and these men come with a fire extinguisher.

If you're still reading after all of that then, by all means, sit down, relax, and enjoy the filthy, bumpy road ahead.

To reiterate:

***!! If you have triggers, please do not continue. This is not the series for you. !!***

Seriously, if you don't want all the angst and smut with some suspenseful darkness thrown in for good measure, stop reading.

**Did you stop?**

**No?**

**Ooh, we like you, you rebel!**

To Henry Cavil, Jason Momoa, Tom Hardy, Keanu Reeves, Chris Hemsworth... (You get the gist) Thank you for existing and giving us some excellent spank bank material.

And of course...

To the three people who know who we are. You're the best and we love you.

# CHAPTER ONE

## RIVER

"**G**et on your knees, you worthless piece of shit."

The shower isn't very big, but there's enough room for the guy I'm pegging to turn around, get on his knees and kneel at my feet. He stares up at me with lust-filled eyes as I grab the sides of his face and position myself over him.

And then I let it out. I pee all over his hair like I'm giving him a shower—which I am. A golden one. Groans of pleasure erupt from him as he palms his dick, roughly tugging at it before he spurts all over his hand just as I dry up.

"Good boy." After helping him stand, I turn the shower on, full and hot. Cleanliness is essential when engaging in watersports. I'm careful with my wig because getting it wet would kill my client's fantasy.

He doesn't speak as he scrubs his tanned, athletic body, but that's not unusual for him. This is the third time I've seen him in the last three years. Always on the same day, always the same request, always the same humiliation. This guy is definitely broken.

Stepping out of the shower, he wraps his waist with a fluffy dark-blue towel before grabbing my pink one and folding it around me. I always bring my own since it's the only way to guarantee it hasn't been spunked on before I rub it all over my body. Past experience has taught me a few things, and bringing my own towel is one of them.

"Thank you, *Rose*. Can I book you in for the same time next year, please?" His complete submissive demeanor has faded now that we're dressed, his tailored Armani suit giving back some of his power. Though he still holds an air of shyness to him. My background check on him told me he works for his dad, something dealing with finance. He's a private person, the most I've ever heard him speak was at his first booking when we briefly discussed what he wanted, rules, and safe words. Since then, he's usually waiting on his knees at the foot of the hotel room bed before I arrive, and his only words are "yes, miss" when I demand them—and his request to book his next appointment.

"Of course, John. I'll schedule you in, and we can arrange the location via email a little closer to the date of our next meeting." He nods in agreement as I grab my small travel bag full of goodies and wheel it to the door. He doesn't look like a John, but then again, I guess I don't look like a Rose, either. I know he's using an alias just like I am, but at three-thousand dollars for a couple of hours, I'll call him the fucking Easter bunny if that's what gets him off.

This isn't the life I would have chosen for myself. It's not like I dreamed of being a call girl while playing with my Barbie dolls. I didn't write essays at school about fucking men for cash as my end goal. In fact, I didn't even go to school. My hippie parents wouldn't allow it, and my brother and I were home-schooled.

No matter how free-loving my family was, I still never imagined my life going in this direction.

Yet, here I am.

Do I regret it? I probably should. However, every time I see the happiness on my brother Everest's face, I suck it up and tell myself there's a reason for everything.

I suppose my only respite is that I still get to choose who I fuck. Nobody has a hold on me except for my guilt. Even that is a rarity.

I don't bother with a drawn-out goodbye. There really is no need. I tilt my head slightly in his direction to indicate we're done here as I open the door and walk out. Leaving him to meticulously tie his shoes.

As the door clicks shut behind me, I wonder—and not for the first time—what the hell happened to this man, to this brown-eyed Greek God? People aren't born dark and broken, life makes them this way.

The cool night air hits my bare legs as I step outside of the hotel, my knee-length coat keeping the worst of the chill from reaching the rest of my body. The walk home should only take about twenty minutes, but Louboutin's are not made for walking that kind of distance on these New York streets, especially not at night.

Hailing the first available cab, I ask the driver to stop at my favorite taco place on the way. Food always helps me sleep easier after a long, adrenaline-fueled evening. I promised my brother I'd help him and his wife, Petal, unpack and get settled into their new little suburban house in Staten Island tomorrow morning, so tonight is going to be exceptionally short and I need all the sleep I can get. He's lucky I love them. I wouldn't get up at five in the morning for anyone else. Unless they were paying me of course.

He's also lucky our fine-ass best friend, Kai, is going to be helping out.

Taco in hand, I step out of the cab, pay the driver, close the door, and am greeted by Mr. Bobby's smiling face. The man is basically a fixture of the old and crumbling building, sitting at his usual spot on the stoop and watching the comings and goings of everyone in the neighborhood. He lives on the bottom floor of our building and is fifty years my senior, but I won't deny having sat with him a few times to watch the world go by with something a little stronger than the coffee he usually drinks.

"Evening, Mr. Bobby." I give a little finger wave in greeting.

"Evening to you too, my girl. Where is your gentleman friend and why isn't he seeing you to your door?" The smirk on his face and the crinkle in his eyes do little to hide his amusement. He often tells me I need to find a nice young man to settle down and have kids with before I get too old. Which is laughable—I'm only twenty-six, and I have no desire to have children. Every time I come home late, he asks these questions, trying to get me to spill all my secrets. It never works, but he seems to enjoy trying. It's kind of our thing.

"He had to rush off on a secret mission to Mars, so he shoved me in a cab and sent me on my way." He shakes his head and rolls his brown eyes at me as I can't keep a straight face. "Anyway, what are you still doing out here at this time of night? It's almost nine-thirty. You're usually settled in your apartment by now."

"Ah, don't mind me, I was just finishing up my coffee. Come on, I'll head inside with you."

"I'll even hold the door for you." I give him a quick side hug, ruffle the small amount of white hair on top of his head and pull the door open before following him inside the building.

Finally taking off my wig as I step inside my apartment is one of the most satisfying things a girl can experience—even more than taking my shoes off, but not as much as multiple orgasms. My head suddenly feels lighter, and I'm no longer Rose. I'm River again. Not that Mr. Bobby ever notices, he is used to my ever-changing hair by now. I finish off my taco before stripping and taking another steaming hot shower, washing my short hair this time too.

As much as showering with my clients gets me clean, it doesn't compare to the quiet moment of solitude where I can wash my work day away. Although a long shower with Kai is equally satisfying. Our first time together, he took such good care of me afterward. Taking the time to massage my head as he washed my hair, caressing my soapy body with his huge work-worn hands, placing gentle kisses all over me and expecting nothing in return. A shower always feels so clinical with my clients, but with Kai, it was nothing short of Heaven.

It wasn't long after this that we decided neither of us were in the right headspace to be together properly, and the way he unknowingly broke my heart before that moment was still ingrained into my brain. I mean, this hasn't stopped us fucking around since then, but that's all it ever is.

Once I'm dried off and wearing my favorite unicorn jammies, I lie on my bed, and allow my thoughts to drift again. Tomorrow should be fun. It's been a hot minute since I've seen Kai, and I can't say I'm not looking forward to it.

I'm about to doze off when the flashing light from my phone drags me back into consciousness. It's an unknown number on my work phone but I'm too tired to deal with clients tonight.

It didn't take me long to get ready this morning, just a little eyeliner and lip-gloss, along with my denim overall shorts and a large flannel shirt. My hair was easy, I just swept it all to one side before sliding my feet into my Timberlands... with heels—as if there was any doubt.

At five in the morning, there were plenty of seats available on the subway, and even more on the ferry. Everest picked me up from the terminal, and even that early, he was already high as a kite. Which means I couldn't get him to shut the fuck up. The best part of my morning so far was seeing Kai for the first time in too long.

I expected him to be here, but Christ, I almost forgot how utterly delicious he looks. Especially wearing the holy grail of all male clothing—gray sweatpants. I'm used to seeing him in jeans or cargo pants with Henley tops or a flannel. This is definitely new, and I won't say I hate it.

"Only you would wear Timbs with fucking heels on them to help someone move." The deep timber of his voice vibrates through my entire body. Such a dickhead.

"I can delegate in six-inch stilettos without even moving my little finger. Move your ass, you're in my way." With a side smile, I raise an eyebrow and place a hand on my hip, tilting my head as I wait for him to let me pass through to the kitchen.

He balances the box he's carrying in one hand to give me a mocking salute, a wink, and a trademark grin before heading upstairs. I love how he reacts to my sass. Anyone else would assume I was being shitty with them, but not him.

The day is spent making more cups of coffee than I can count. Petal and I pretty much left the guys to do most of the actual unpacking while we sat back and ogled them. After lunch, we cracked open the wine and we're now five glasses in with stupid smiles on our faces.

"Do you think one more cup of coffee would get them to take their shirts off? I can see the sweat on Ev's head, he's got to be close to stripping down." Petal sniggers before finishing off her glass and pouring us both some more.

"Eww. Let's be clear, I'm only helping so I can watch Kai. I have no desire to see my brother's abs. Just no." Mocking a disgusted look on my face, I exaggerate a shiver, causing Petal to roll her eyes at me. "See what just the thought did?!" She stares at me, her brown eyes wide, before we both burst into a fit of giggles. My abs hurt, we've laughed so much. We should really think about ordering some food soon, seeing as it's almost eight and we all need to eat.

"What are you girls laughing about? Did Petal show you a pic of Ev's new ass tat?" Kai's voice sends flutters in between my legs, and I'm consciously ignoring the butt tattoo thing. I don't wanna know.

"Fuck off, dude." Ev slaps Kai in the back of the head as he follows him into the kitchen.

"Hey, baby, want me to take out the cold beers?" Petal drapes herself over him, her long blond hair falling over her shoulder as she nestles her nose into his neck and pauses. "Why can I smell whiskey?" She's not pissed, just curious.

"We might've been spiking our coffees." His smirk and the glaze in his eyes tells me he's dialing down his intake.

"Is that weed? Oh, Ev! I can't believe you two went out for a smoke without inviting us. Rude."

I miss what else is said as they exit the room and Kai invades my space. Placing his strong arms to either side of my hips on the counter behind me, he cages me in. I can smell the alcohol and weed on his breath too. Not the best combination, but his honeyed eyes and those freaking dimples overpower everything else. He used to hate them when we were younger, but now, combined with his dark stubble, he's nothing less than breathtaking.

As far as I'm concerned those dimples will be my downfall.

"Kai, what are you doing?" My voice sounds husky, my breathing heavier than I'd like as I look up into his eyes. We've got a complicated past, and even though we've never dated, there's always been something there. Just looking at him takes me back to a time where anything and everything was possible.

"Just saying hi, *Psyche*. I haven't really talked to you all day." He doesn't break eye contact as he speaks, and I swear his arms look like they're about to burst out of the black t-shirt he's wearing. He's using the nickname we came up with as kids, when we pinky-promised each other we'd get married one day. We would spend hours gazing at the stars as he told me stories of the Gods, deciding I was Psyche, the most beautiful of all the mortals, and he was Eros—A.K.A. Cupid—Psyche's beloved husband. The nostalgic feeling that nickname gives me is warming, but we were just kids then. We've both grown up and are living our separate lives, only seeing each other now and then like ships passing in the night. To be fair, our emotional distance the last few years has been on me.

With the life choices I've had to make since then, keeping that childhood promise is impossible. Maybe once upon a time it could've worked out between us. As much as we seem to be drawn to each other, I can't risk seeing the look on his face when he finds out what I do. Too much has happened and we just have to live with those choices.

"Would your girlfriend like it if you were saying hi to me like this, Kai?" One of his past flings flooded my inbox with death threats after seeing us together at one of my brother's dinner parties. So what if we'd hooked up in the bathroom...? I felt a bit sorry for her, but she was a crazy bitch anyway, and they were nothing more than a one-night stand. Apparently she didn't get the memo, but that has nothing to do with me and I really don't need something like that happening again.

"We've been over for weeks now." The glint in his eye says so much, yet nothing at all.

"What happened?" Butterflies erupt in my lower belly as he leans in and runs the tip of his nose up my jawline. The smell of him is intoxicating.

"She wasn't you."

"Kai..."

"Mmm, jasmine. My favorite." He lifts me onto the counter and nudges my legs apart, standing himself in between them.

"What do you know about jasmine?" I raise a challenging eyebrow, my voice barely a whisper, trying to keep the moment light and failing miserably. Inside though, I'm burning.

For him.

For us.

For everything we could have been.

"It's what you wear, and that's all I need to know." As he lowers his face to mine, our gazes lock, and my fucking cellphone rings, cutting through the building tension. At first Kai doesn't move. He smirks and flashes those god-damn dimples at me again before moving to stand beside me and giving me space to answer my phone.

"Hello?"

Nothing.

Silence.

I look at the screen and realize it's another unknown number, just like last night. This isn't the first time and it probably won't be the last. I had been warned that in my profession, strange phone calls come with the territory, but these last few days it's ramped up and is seriously pissing me off.

"Hello?"

And then it starts. The heavy breathing, as if someone is jacking himself off, lasting mere seconds before there's a blood-curdling scream.

# CHAPTER TWO

## RIVER

"**W**hat the fuck was that, River?" I blink as Kai's voice pierces through the fog of my thoughts. Great fucking question.

The first thought that crosses my mind is that my work phone is compromised. Prank calls are expected, but this feels different. Ice shot up my spine as that scream pierced through the line.

Or maybe one of my clients has gone fucking insane?

Either way, something is definitely wrong. Problem is, I *cannot* talk to Kai about it or else he'll have a complete meltdown. Fuck, I wish our circumstances were different.

We aren't a couple, but the bond between us has always been strong, the chemistry pulling us together every time we're in the same vicinity. It's been a problem for us in the past; girlfriends jealous of me, boyfriends going crazy over my friendship with him. We've always laughed about it, but the truth of the matter is that any chance we get, we end up fucking like teenagers in places no one should be fucking.

If my brother knew how many times I've ridden our best friend, he'd probably have a stroke. I mean, he's all about free love and all that shit but when it comes to his big sister, Everest is akin to a papa bear.

"Wrong number." I turn to him, and if I weren't so used to it, I'd wither under his piercing gaze. In any circumstance, Kai Briggs is intense. Hair the color of coal, sun-kissed skin from years working construction, and his eyes—my dear heart, his eyes—are his most addicting feature. Sweet honey when he's feeling playful, but when he's pissed they turn to a rich, aged whiskey that burns right through you.

Right now, he's scorching.

"There was a scream, River." Cocking a brow like he knows I'm lying, he leans in even closer and the scent of him makes me wet in an instant. Sandalwood and sweat with a hint of whiskey.

His closeness is so overwhelming that I almost forget the weird phone call. I ignore the bells and alarms in my brain telling me to move away, reminding me that Kai and I...? We're not destined to be together, despite what our six-year-old selves promised. He's the boy next door looking for marriage and two-point-three kids, living a quiet life out in Staten Island. PTA meetings and Saturday practice for the lucky soccer moms who can ogle him in all his fatherly glory.

I'm an escort. A prostitute. A fucking whore. Our ship sailed the day he broke my heart and didn't even realize it.

"Then it was a prank. You were here, Kai. You know just as much about it as I do." I take shallow breaths to avoid inhaling him fully.

I once read that sandalwood is a powerful aphrodisiac, and even used for self-arousal. I love that. The idea that we can be turned on by our own scent. The problem is that being around Kai intoxicates me no matter what scent is wafting from him. I don't even mind the weed. His entire presence elicits a desire in me that always has me wanting to fuck him for hours.

I startle at the gentle touch of his finger against my temple as he guides an errant strand of hair behind my ear.

"I miss you." His words are like a blanket over my senses—muting my self-control—and I have no idea where I get the strength to resist him.

"Don't. We're not good for each other, Kai. You know this." Swatting his hand away, I clear my throat, shove against his rock-hard chest, and slide down from the counter. I need to be standing in order to keep my wits about me.

"The hell we're not. I'm Eros and you're Psyche. We're fucking destined." I allow my gaze a few seconds to run over his sharp features. His strong, Roman nose, the slash of dominant brows, and his eyes that have turned the color of temptation.

Because I'm me and he's him, I lean in—one hand at the back of his head—and kiss him with every desire I've ever had. Our lips crash together like they always do, our tongues dancing in muscle memory. Around the kitchen, our light moans bounce off the walls before I retreat just enough to whisper against his mouth. "There's no such thing as destiny." Taking in a fortifying breath, I fix him with my green gaze, presenting him with my "Rose" mask; the face I give my clients to avoid any attachments. The hard exterior he doesn't deserve.

I don't take two steps away before one of Kai's arms is around my waist and pulling me back against the wall of his work-honed chest. "Liar." He drops a soft kiss against the column of my neck, and I feel the tip of his tongue against his favorite beauty mark before he lets me go.

Just when I think I'm going to give in to him—again—my brother walks back in and makes the decision for me.

"Dude, I'm starving." We both startle, and by the confusion written all over Everest's face, there's no doubt we look guilty.

"You're always starving." Kai's right, my brother is a bottomless pit when it comes to food. Yet he's never put on a single pound that isn't hard-earned muscle.

Thankfully, the rest of the evening goes by in a bit of an intoxicated blur, but the light sizzle between Kai and I never completely dissipates.

Early the next morning, Kai drives me back to the ferry. He's his usual carefree self and apart from kissing my temple and lingering a second too long, our time together is uneventful. As I wait to board, thoughts of two kids lying under the infinity of the star-filled sky run through my mind. Nine-year-old Kai holding my hand as he recounted the stories of Greek Gods.

*"For centuries, Aphrodite was the center of attention among the mortals. She was beautiful and strong and everyone loved her. Then one day, all of that attention was focused on Psyche, because she was suddenly the most beautiful creature on Earth."* Squeezing my hand, he turns to me and whispers. *"Like you, River."*

The memory nearly destroys me yet again. How did we get to this place? In the last few years, Kai is the only man I've fucked as River. As myself. He's the only one who knows me, knows who I am beneath the stilettos and wigs.

Still, not even he knows everything. No one does. Not a single person knows the mirrored sides of my persona. They either know me as the relaxed kid of a hippie family or the sultry temptress in six-inch heels.

I'm River. But I'm also Rose. Two sides of the same coin, coexisting but unable to show the entirety of our truth all at once.

My phone rings just as I reach the footpath at St. George terminal to board the ferry, the caller's name splashed across the screen in bold letters. "The Rich One".

Taking a deep breath, I swipe away my childhood memories and make sure Rose is on the line, ready to work.

"Tyler, it's been a while." Tyler Walker is his real name. There is no denying this fact since he's been the constant obsession of *Page Six* in Manhattan. For the last few months, I've been his go-to date when he needs someone on his arm. Our contract states that I use my deep red wig with long ringlets that fall to the middle of my back. It's not that he can't get a date, quite the opposite, really. The onslaught of available women makes him gun shy. I'm his armor, the protection he needs at galas or long weekends in the Hamptons. Although, truth be told, some of those women don't give a damn that he's there with me. If I weren't in the middle of that shit storm, I'd have a blast watching the social experiment from afar.

"Rose, how are you?" He doesn't actually give me the time to answer his question, I figured out it was rhetorical the second time I tried to say I was doing well. "I need you this weekend. A last-minute trip to Martha's Vineyard has been scheduled. Are you available? If not, I'll pay double your fee for you to cancel." I don't have anything scheduled; I try to keep my weekends to myself for a multitude of reasons—Tyler's last-minute bookings being one of them.

"No, I'm free. What do you need?"

"You're a lifesaver. It's one of those hotel garden parties on Saturday evening, but there will be plenty of time for you to relax while I'm in meetings. Bring a swimsuit of your choice and be sure to have at least one casual outfit and one for the outdoor evening party. Bring a shawl, it'll get a little chilly at night." Tyler Walker, business as usual.

"Will do." I smile at the attendant as I make my way to the only row of empty seats. The ferry is jam packed on a Thursday morning as people rush to get to work somewhere in Manhattan. Men and women in suits, children dressed in their private school uniforms... then there's me, playing dress up and making more money in a weekend than most of the people sitting around me make in six months.

"I'll pick you up at your apartment tomorrow around five p.m. Does that work for you?" Looking out at the calm waters of the Hudson Bay, I nod even though he can't see me. It's unusual for a client to know where my real apartment is in Kips Bay, but Tyler's background checks came back clear, and I've been working with him long enough that a modicum of trust has been allowed to blossom between us. It's just convenient for me to have him pick me up there, where all my things are, rather than at my 'work' apartment in Rose Hill.

"Yes." My voice is ever so professional. "That's perfect."

There are no tender words, no pet names or sweet goodbyes. As Rose, I'm all business, and that mentality allows me the freedom to plan for the future as River. It's the reason Everest and Petal could put a down payment on their new house. The reason my living in Manhattan is a possibility.

This weekend, Rose will bring in thirty grand. Five for Friday evening. Fifteen for all of Saturday, and ten for Sunday. Tyler is a very sexual man—his dominance unmistakable—but his end goal isn't about getting his dick wet, although it's rare if he *doesn't* use me to fuck out his frustrations. His reason behind hiring me is to keep his mind on business, always.

An hour later, I walk up the steps of the subway entrance, and land across the street from the little grocery store two blocks away from my studio. It's a mom-and-pop little hole in the wall but it has everything I need; cheese and wine included.

I take the three steps down to the front door where the little bell announces my arrival.

"River, *bella*, how are you?" Running a hand through my short hair to pull it away from my face, I give Francesca a beaming smile and practice my Italian on her. She's been trying to teach me the basics for the last year, but apparently, I do not have the language gene.

"*Buona serata*, Francesca. *Come va*?" I know the words were right but from the expression on Francesca's face, I don't need to be a mind reader to know my accent was shit.

"Ah, now you've done it." The rich timbre of a familiar voice graces my ears and I feel my cheeks burn with heat. Turning, I see one of the store's regular clients who must, apparently, have the same habits I do. At least three times a week, we run into each other at the store. I may choose my drop-in times accordingly but I'll deny it with my last breath.

"Nah, they know I'm a lost cause, but I will keep trying to learn until the end of time."

"*Si*, a lost cause but a good girl." My blush returns with Francesca's most unsubtle attempt at matchmaking.

"Right," Candy Aisle Guy—named conveniently after the place where I first laid eyes on him, between the Skittles and the Nerds—clears his throat and gives me a smile that makes my inner Disney princess melt in a puddle. His rich brown hair mussed from what was evidently a long day, he lowers his gaze and nods politely. He's dressed in jeans and a vee-neck sweater and if it weren't for the Rolex at his wrist and the seven-hundred-dollar Hermès shoes on his feet, I'd say he's just another New Yorker getting his morning orange juice. "I'm sure she's lovely."

Our gazes catch for the briefest of moments before the connection is broken as I force my feet to take me to the back of the store. The ring on his finger tells me everything I need to know. He's flattered, but he's married.

A bottle of wine, a bag of pasta, and some kind of French cheese later, I'm back at the front of the store and trying to remember how the fuck I say the next Italian phrase.

"A little early for wine, isn't it?" The amusement in his voice doesn't escape me but still, the blush heats my cheeks.

"Yeah, but I swear it's for tonight." Biting my lower lip, I realize I'm acting a little coy, which is so far from normal for me that I quickly school my features.

"Dinner for one?" Is he...?

"*Questo è tutto*?" I mentally thank Francesca for the interruption as she asks me if that will be all.

"*Si, grazie. E questo è tutto.*" And it is absolutely all I need. In fact, I do not need another gorgeous, complicated man in my life. Even if it's just at my corner grocer.

"*E molto buono, bella. Bella fatica.* It's very good. Good effort." I level her with a look that says she's a liar but I love her for it.

I turn and say goodbye, my arms wrapped around my paper bag and a little spring in my step when my phone rings again.

I shift the bag onto one arm, fishing out my phone from the pouch at the front of my overalls, and frown at the screen.

Unknown number.

*Motherfucker.*

"Look, I don't know who you are but you need to fuck right off." I barely finish my rant when another scream hits my ears, turning my blood cold. I don't know how my groceries don't fall to the sidewalk. Even more baffling is how I have the wherewithal to take one step after the other all the way to my apartment building. As though on autopilot, I make it to my floor, to my door, I open it, and as I step inside, I turn and lock myself in. First, the top, then the middle, and finally the bottom deadbolt.

Someone is fucking with me and I vow to go to the police first thing tomorrow morning. I'm still hungover and tired from last night's fun, so dealing with this shit today is not on my agenda.

# Chapter Three

## River

I had to rush back from the police station this morning so I had enough time to finish packing for this weekend. Now dressed in a subtle, lightly floral, skater-style dress, and my nude Jimmy Choo's, I make sure my fiery red wig is in place before rolling my Louis Vuitton luggage to the door.

I'm going to need a new work number, which means letting all my regular clients have the information and updating the details on my life-coaching website—which is just a front for what I really do. Annoying as fuck, but if it's going to help stop these weirdo phone calls, I'm all for it.

That's something I can deal with on Monday. Right now, it's time to put Rose in the driver's seat as Tyler Walker's devoted girlfriend for an entire weekend.

My personal phone buzzes in my hand and when I see the name flashing on my screen, a secret smile graces my lips.

**Kai:** Any news on the weird phone call? Don't think I've forgotten about that, Psyche.

**Me:** Aw, are you worried about little ol' me?

**Kai:** Always.

Checking the time confirms Tyler should be rolling up within the next minute. He's extremely prompt, never a minute early or late, which I appreciate.

**Me:** Can't talk right now, catch up later?

**Kai:** River.

I can almost hear his tone—hard and commanding with a dash of worry. But like I said, I can't talk right now.

**Me:** Tada, talk later. *kissy face emoji*

**Kai:** *pleading face emoji* *devil face emoji* *squid emoji* *donut emoji*

**Me:** *woman dancing emoji*

**Kai:** *hand emoji* *peach emoji*

I don't respond to that last one, and I know I'll be paying for that later.

The stoop outside is occupied by none other than Mr. Bobby, slurping on his regular coffee.

"Ooh, you're looking mighty fancy, my girl. Off to anywhere nice?" His white hair glistens in the afternoon sun. He's got a surprising amount of it left for an older man. Something I know his wife loved to grab when she was alive. The woman was a constant barrel full of sexual exploits that she wasn't embarrassed to share with me. It broke my heart the day she died, and although Mr. Bobby doesn't show it, it changed his whole world. This is just one reason I vowed to her spirit that I would always look out for him, even though he thinks he's the one looking out for me.

"Hey, Mr. Bobby. I'm just going to Martha's Vineyard for the weekend with a friend."

"A boyfriend?" The glint in his eyes makes me laugh. I can't help it. He's like the endearing old grandpa that sits in the corner telling crude jokes at family parties.

A sleek, black SUV pulls up before I can answer. Not that I was going to be honest, but I hate lying to Mr. Bobby, so it's always nice when I don't have to.

"Looks like my ride's here. I'll be home on Sunday evening at some point. Have a great weekend." I kiss him on the cheek before rolling my luggage over to the Lincoln Navigator, handing it over to Aaron—Tyler's driver—who stands waiting to put it in the trunk.

Tyler greets me with a head nod as I get into the back of the SUV, his phone to his ear so I know not to speak. Gesturing to the champagne-filled glasses sitting on the little table in front of us, he silently invites me to help myself. I don't usually drink while I'm working, but the occasional glass is allowed. I've had a busy few days, and I deserve a nice cold glass of liquid gold. Besides, there's enough trust between us that I can let my barriers down just a tiny fraction.

After a few sips, Tyler finishes with his call, placing his phone into the inside pocket of his designer suit jacket. I've got to admit, he is easy on the eyes. The dark gray suit does wonders for his well-toned body, the white collared shirt setting off his tanned skin beautifully. He's slightly more casual today with no tie and the top button of his shirt undone. Something most girls would drool over. Definitely a walking wet dream. But he's my client, and getting attached goes against our contract and my general life rules.

"I have a schedule for the weekend here for you, Rose. I have no doubt you'll be perfect as usual. This weekend is going to be a little different than the others. It'll be the first time I've seen Cora since she left." His deep brown eyes are downcast as he speaks, the shame he feels from the cliché of his wife cheating on him with his best friend—and business partner—is evident.

The subject of Cora has come up a few times, late at night, when the moon is high and in the safety of darkness. In those moments, I'm not just a sex toy, I'm an unbiased confidant. Cora and his best friend have been in Dubai since I've known him, and he knew she was coming back soon, I'm just not so sure he was prepared for it being now.

He clears his throat before speaking again. "I bought you a new dress for the party tomorrow night. I'm sure whatever you had planned would've been fine, but this dress is the statement I want to make."

"Of course, no problem." He passes me the schedule with a nod before pulling out his phone again.

The start of the evening didn't go as planned for Tyler. His business partner, Brett, arrived earlier than planned and immediately started schmoozing some of their clients. I know this pissed him off, the agitation in his features as he handed our luggage over to the concierge of the Harbor

View Hotel was clear. It was quickly masked as he took a deep breath and led me into the Edgartown Room.

It's beautifully set up; cylindrical white pillars spaced throughout the room, interspersed with a few rectangular ones with mirrors on all four sides; panoramic views of the harbor and the iconic lighthouse through large windows along two walls, with equally large glass doors leading out onto the veranda. We've been here for an hour so far, with me attached to Tyler's arm, ever the doting girlfriend. Nodding and smiling, laughing at the most boring jokes in the world so his clients think they're funny.

"Why don't you go and get us both a drink, Rose. I've just got something to talk with Joshua about, and I'll meet you on the veranda." He wraps his arm around my waist and pulls me in to kiss the top of my head.

"Of course, I'll see you out there." A wink and a smile in his direction, clear for *Joshua* to see, and I turn on my heel and head toward the bar—a little extra wiggle in my step for good measure. Tyler likes to make his clients jealous, says it takes them off guard just enough to get what he wants out of them. Not that I know exactly what that entails. We may talk, but it's never about business.

On our first appointment, I decided he was the money man for an important mobster. I know that's way off base, he actually runs a chain of department stores, but being a mobster is much more exciting than the truth. Coming up with fake occupations for my clients makes me feel like an international woman of mystery.

Breathing in the fresh ocean scents as I stand on the veranda is wonderful. It's so peaceful out here. Sounds of people drinking and laughing inside float through the open doors, but it's comforting in a way. Life is happening all around, and here I am in one of the most peaceful places I could imagine.

"That dress isn't exactly formal-drinks attire." The nasally voice comes from behind me, followed by the guffaw of another.

Turning to face them, I steel my nerves, making sure it's Rose who greets them—River would likely punch the rude bitch in the face. Ugh, it's Cora and one of the other rich-bitch wives I've met this evening. They're all so up their own asses it's unreal. I swear they should all have brown lipstick on to match the shit coming out of their mouths.

"Oh, this?" I feign a nervous laugh. "We arrived a little late. Had to stop on the way because... well..." I look down as if I'm embarrassed. "You know, we had to send the driver away for half an hour for some privacy." Covering my mouth with my hand and looking at them from under my lashes is my final move. Cora is steaming, redness creeping up her chest underneath her barely-there maxi-dress. I smile internally.

"You know you've got my sloppy leftovers, don't you? So I don't know what you're so smug about." She folds her arms over her chest, pushing up her rock-hard breasts that Tyler probably paid for when they were together.

"If you ever slept with him, then you should know exactly what I'm smug about. Right?" I give her my biggest, friendliest smile and hold my hand up for a high five. She is not amused. Oh, but holy fuck, I am!

"Right. It won't be long until he gets bored of you. Remember this conversation on the third or fourth night he hasn't come home because of..." She pauses, leans in slightly, and hooks her fingers in the air quoting her last word, enunciating it like a plague. "Business."

"Is that your version of the events, Cora? Funny, I remember coming home and finding you fucking my best friend. Tomayto, tomahto." Tyler approaches her from behind. Of course I saw him coming, but fuck if I was going to tell her that.

She looks flustered as he walks around her and grabs the back of my neck, pulling me in for a panty-melting kiss. All teeth and tongues, dirty, just how he likes it. It's not, however, how he likes to kiss in front of his clients or colleagues; in front of them, he's much more reserved. This is him putting on a show for Cora, and I'm happy to oblige.

I hear some huffs and high-pitched mumbles, but I'm not really paying attention to anything apart from Tyler. Exactly what he pays me for.

When he pulls away, Cora and her little snot-nosed friend have gone. "Are you okay?" I love that he's concerned about my interaction with his ex, it's uncharacteristically sweet.

"I'm good, Tyler. Nothing I can't handle. She's jealous, so I'd say job well done." I grin at him as he continues to hold me, one arm around my waist, the other still behind my head. To anyone watching from afar, we look like any other couple in love.

"Job well done indeed, Rose. Come on, let's go to our room. I've had enough of everyone in there for tonight." Closing his eyes, he tilts his face to the sky and takes a deep breath, as if steeling himself to walk back through the room full of his clients and colleagues. I can imagine everyone wanting a piece of your time all day every day is grating.

The hotel room is simple, but elegant. A huge bed full of pillows in the center of the room, a padded bench at the end of it, and French doors showing a beautiful view of the harbor. It's stunning. I don't have a lot of time to look around though. Tyler is ready. The brief interaction with Cora is likely what has him so worked up.

"Shower, now." After traveling all day, I really don't hate this idea.

I strip with slow, practiced seduction, holding his gaze before padding through to the bathroom, looking at him over my shoulder as I move. This is all part of the performance for him. He sometimes likes to clean us both before and after. All part of his control fantasy.

"Every man in that room wanted to fuck you, tonight." Rubbing slow circles of soap over my body, he takes his time on my nipples, sliding down and pausing to squeeze my ass.

Naked, he is beautiful to look at, as if Michelangelo himself was responsible for sculpting this stunning man. Dips in all the right places, muscles glistening under the warm spray of water.

"But I'm the lucky bastard who gets to watch you come all over my dick."

He flicks his tongue over my left nipple as his fingers delve straight into my pussy, then sucks and nips for a few minutes of torturous pleasure. Quickly removing his fingers, he gets on his knees and washes my legs and feet, keeping most of his attention nearest the tops of my thighs, rubbing along my creases and folds multiple times.

A slap on my ass is the only warning that he's done here, as the glass door is opened and Tyler grabs a couple of fluffy white towels—for the price of this room, I think I can trust them. After first wrapping one around his waist, he pulls the other around my shoulders, and takes his time making sure I'm dry. Everywhere.

I know what he wants next, so once he's finished, I pad through to the bedroom, drop the towel at my feet and get on all fours. A grunt Geralt from *The Witcher* would be proud of escapes his lips as he climbs on the bed behind me. Immediately burying his face into me, his tongue flicks at my clit like it's his last meal.

This alone could bring me to orgasm, but I hold off for just a little longer. He may be paying for it, but there's nothing to say I can't enjoy myself at the same time.

The addition of his fingers, curling and hitting that delicious sweet spot, sends me over the edge, and he laps up my juices like a pro before standing. With no time to get over my orgasm, I'm a little floaty as I turn my body so my face is level with his cock. Looking up at him through my lashes, I lick the underside of it and pop the tip in my mouth, flicking over the slit with my tongue and sucking the head like a strawberry lollipop.

He moans as he grabs the back of my head, always mindful that it's a wig I'm wearing so he never pulls too hard. He guides me up and down his shaft, bottoming out and hitting the back of my throat. My eyes water as I gag on the length of him, but I breathe through my nose, ever the professional.

As he gets close, he pulls out and wipes the spit on the side of my mouth away with his thumb, before grabbing a condom from the bedside table and rolling it on.

"Turn around. Ass up." The lust in his voice is unmistakable. He's so close, this won't take long at all. I hope he lasts long enough for me to have another orgasm.

I shift to rest my elbows and knees on the bed, arching my back and putting my ass on show for him. This is his favorite position. He spits onto my ass hole, rubbing it around and down over my clit, before lining himself up with my pussy. He nudges in slowly at first, gripping my hips and pulling me onto him. Once he's fully seated, he lets out a groan of relief. A slap on my ass is the only warning I get, as he begins to thrust in and out of me like a wild animal.

"Your ass looks good with my handprint on it." Another slap, on the other cheek this time. All things we've agreed were acceptable before we even had our first appointment. We both have a safe word if ever needed.

"Harder, Tyler. Fuck me harder." I'm panting, my building orgasm better come soon, because I know he's really close. The increasing sting on my ass says as much.

He reaches around and starts to play with my nipple, pinching and twisting, giving me just the right amount of pain with my pleasure. His other hand leaves my hip, squeezing my ass as his thumb gets closer to my ass hole. I feel him spit onto it again before he starts rubbing his thumb all over, getting it nice and wet before he puts it inside me. Again, he does this slowly, starting with the tip first. As he does this, his thrusts slow down slightly, and he's pushing his cock so deep inside me I can feel every hard ridge.

I push myself back onto him, enticing him, seeking out more—faster. He keeps his thumb in my ass, and moves his other hand back to grab my hip, squeezing painfully as he gets frantic, even more animalistic than before, all rhythm gone.

"Yes! Fuck, yes!" I don't even need to exaggerate my screams as he pounds into me harder. He's an exceptional lover, and for that, I'm lucky. It's easy to make him feel like a king when he treats me like a queen and fucks me like a whore, multiple orgasms and all.

A loud grunt is my first indication he's coming, as well as the erratic way he thrusts into me. I don't mind though. One more of those hard pumps and the sensation of another orgasm rolls through me. Our slapping bodies slow down as we both breathe heavily, small moans of pleasure escaping our mouths.

After cleaning up, Tyler climbs back into bed, and I decide to take a minute out on the balcony to cool down and check my phones. It's a beautiful night for sitting outside, the stars clear in the dark sky. I wish I'd paid more attention to Kai's ramblings about the constellations when we were younger, but I was too busy basking in the sound of his voice and the warmth of him beside me as we lay under the stars.

I've got several messages on my work phone that are easily dealt with, so I go through those first. Once I'm finished, I pick up my personal phone, hoping to clear my mind with some mind-numbing, world building game. I have a whole land of dragons I've been growing for the last six months. I lose all sense of time as I play, but the flashing message icon makes me pause. There are only a few people who have this number, and I'm not expecting to hear from any of them this weekend.

I open my messages, curious, and my fingers freeze. My breath seizes for half a second as I read the unexpected words.

"Oh shit."

# Chapter Four
## River

"Is everything all right?" My breath catches at the sound of Tyler's voice so close behind me. Spinning around like a kid caught stealing the last of the candy in the cupboard, I slam a hand to my heart and force a smile on my lips. No need to alarm the billionaire client.

"Oh crap, you scared me!" I take in his mussed brown hair and lean frame as one hand scratches the back of his head. For the first time, he doesn't exude the potent vibe of the owner of half the state. Possibly the country. No, for the first time, I see the man. The mere mortal who has woken up a little disoriented. It's gone quickly enough, like a wall building right before my eyes.

"Light sleeper," is all he says as he steps closer, dark chocolate eyes roaming my body, my face, and then landing on my lips for a second too long. "What are you doing out here?" His voice sounds distracted. It's then I realize, his gaze is locked on my hair.

"Light sleeper." I use his own words on him and grace him with a genuine smile. His hand reaches out to touch me and I fight the urge to flinch. Not a lot of people know what my true hair looks like. Mostly because I'm always in character with my clients. Besides going out for some nearby shopping within a three or four block area, the only place I ever go without a wig is Staten Island to see my brother and Petal. But I trust Tyler to a certain extent and—as much as I am capable—because I know he has even more to lose than I do.

"Touché." Toying with some errant strands that fall across one of my eyes, I watch him as his gaze follows the movement of his fingers. "I forgot that your hair is so dark and short. I'm so used to seeing you with the long red hair that it takes a minute to remember." There's something so vulnerable about him right now. Wistful. Like he's standing here but his mind is years away. "I like it. Short, I mean. It suits you, you know? It says you're strong and resilient." I smile because what else am I supposed to do? This type of conversation makes me uncomfortable. He's my client, I don't want to get to know him or receive compliments when no one else is around. Secretly though, I welcome his praise.

But then the moment is gone. His vulnerability disappears. His eyes darken and his jaw sets.

Billionaire Tyler is back and I can't help but feel the relief.

"We should go inside." His gaze scans the surrounding area, to the sides and below us, before he takes my hand and leads me into the room. "I don't want anyone to see you like this." He throws a grin over his shoulder that can only be described as sardonic. "Wouldn't want anyone accusing me of cheating on my girlfriend."

We both chuckle, and it doesn't escape me that this moment right here is the very definition of cynical.

This is my life.

Trying not to get my fake boyfriend in trouble for fake dating a real prostitute.

Prostitute. I used to cringe at the word, but now I just put on my armor and remind myself of why I'm doing this. Why I can't stop. Not now.

Tyler walks into the lush bathroom and just as he closes the door, I quickly take my phone out and reread the text message I'd misunderstood earlier.

— We need to talk... Rose.

*Fuck.*

By the time I hear the flush of the toilet and the water from the sink, I slip my phone back into my clutch and—heart beating a staggering staccato—slide between the crisp sheets of the hotel bed.

This isn't a cheap motel on the side of the highway. The sheets are clearly Egyptian cotton, if the softness is any indication, with most likely a thread count around six hundred. I'd *almost* bet my weekend's salary on it. I'm not disappointed, that's for sure.

"Do you mind if I keep the side light on? I'm going to work a little." I stretch across his hard chest to check the time on his watch.

"It's almost one in the morning. Don't you need to sleep?" Cocking a brow at me, he lightly shakes his head like my question is ridiculous, but then I remember...

"You're a light sleeper in all the ways, aren't you?" It's a rhetorical question. My chest aches for this man as the loneliness he must feel becomes so damn clear. He's gorgeous—more so than any man has the right to be—with a body that makes all the ladies drop their panties just so they can cream on his cock. Yet, when I look at him, it's his dry sense of humor and genuine kindness toward those he deems worthy that earns my respect. Hell, the cynical part in me half expects his money alone to keep him warm with a willing body in his bed.

But that's just it, isn't it? He's lonely because his money has made him cautious. He's lonely because his money attracts the vultures when he's looking for his penguin.

Well, that and his incredibly stupid ex-wife. What a fucking idiot.

"You deserve better than this. Than me." I slink back to my side of the bed. I'm not putting myself down, I know my worth and it's not defined by my choice in profession, but he deserves more than just a fake anything. He deserves real. All the fucking time.

In a move so quick I barely have time to get my bearings, I'm pushed into the mattress by a very hard, very angry Tyler, whose next words bring a smile to my lips.

"I never pegged you for the self-pitying kind." I'm almost offended, but I get it.

"No, I—" I don't get the chance to explain. A hot, demanding mouth is on mine—lips searching and tongue dominating—and without a thought, I let him take control. It's what he needs. Tyler needs to be in control of his life, of sex, of every fucking thing. Handing it over is my job, literally in the contract that we signed. Also in the contract is the expressed "back off" clause. Any verbal or non-verbal expression of disinterest is to be taken seriously on the spot.

I spread my legs to allow the space for his body to fit. With one of his hands braced at the side of my head, the other pushes his boxers off with the ease and finesse of a cat, his lips never parting with mine.

Usually, I have to put my acting skills to work. I have to give them the feeling they're the best lover on this side of the Atlantic. Usually, I have to take my mind to the place that is my pleasure, my fantasy.

*Kai.*

He has always been my safe space, my could have been. The dream I don't dare voice.

Tyler pushes my legs further apart, his fingers easily sliding into my cunt. My wetness is a welcome discovery if his growl means anything. My clients love it when I'm wet, it gives them the impression that I'm loving what they're doing. That despite my hefty paycheck at the end of the night or the weekend, my body wants them. It's an elaborate lie, all part of my job.

It's called lube, boys.

Except, I wasn't expecting tonight. I'd lubed up before we had sex earlier but not for now and yet here I am, wet as fuck, and it does something to him. Tyler is one of the rare clients who knows I prepare. We've talked about it, laughed about the fact that I shouldn't have to need that with him.

But I insist. I'd hate for my mind to wander and have my pussy dry up like a well in the California deserts.

Not the case right now.

"You look surprised." I yelp as his free hand latches onto the back of my head, fingers curling around the short strands—tightening to the point of pain. "I know how to make a woman come, Rose." His two fingers curl deep inside me, pulling an unsolicited groan from me. When I open my eyes, the self-satisfied grin on his face makes me chuckle.

"Happy?" My voice sounds strange to my ears, like gravel has taken temporary residence in my throat.

Pressing his palm against the opening of my pussy, he rubs his fingers against my g-spot while his palm rubs my clit with laser-like precision.

"I'll be happy when you come so loudly that my ex-wife regrets spreading her treacherous legs for another man." His words are a cold shower. A stark reminder of why I'm here. Of what I do. Of why he's paying me.

I don't skip a beat, I raise my hips and push into his hand, grunting at all the right times, making him feel like the powerful man he is.

And he will make me come loud enough to be heard next door. I'll make sure of it.

Men like Tyler thrive on their self-control, on their dominance. They need to feel the power of their decisions, to know their life choices are justified.

A cheating wife was like a kick to the balls, and from what I hear, they hurt like a fucking cunt on a power trip.

I belt out a moan that could make the most popular of porn stars feel insignificant.

"Don't you fucking dare, Rose. You moan because I make you fucking moan. You don't moan because I pay you to do it."

*Fuck*.

We both still, gazes locked in a battle of wills as he dares me to disobey him. This can't be good for business.

"Tyler—"

"Let's make a deal." He must see the confusion written all over my face. We're both naked, two of his fingers are up my pussy, another hand controlling the angle of my head, and he wants to negotiate?

"Forget I'm paying you. For the next twenty minutes, let me bring you pleasure. Look at it as a bonus for the incredible job you do for me and for putting up with my fucked up moods." I stare at him for a minute—which is a really fucking long time with two unmoving fingers inside me.

"You want to make me come? Again?" I arch a brow, a challenge in my features.

"Yes." Simple and to the point.

"And if you can't? I mean, twenty minutes isn't nearly enough time for me to get myself off, so..." I trail off, hoping he can fill in the blanks.

He pulls my head closer to his mouth, a power play if I've ever seen one. Instead of leaning into me, he brings me to him.

"Fifteen, then." His words are murmured against my lips, the challenge in them an aphrodisiac. It's been so long since sex was actually fun and unpredictable that I grin up at him and shrug like it makes absolutely no difference to me either way.

It's a fucking lie.

I'm intrigued.

Orgasms are a tricky thing. Not necessarily impossible, I've already had two tonight, but not snap-your-fingers available, either, and the mention of his ex-wife kind of put a fire out in my libido.

"If I lose, I'll double your pay for this weekend." I draw in a sharp breath. Double? Jesus, I could put a major dent in Everest's student loans, as well as the mortgage on his house.

My face must show my answer because a slow, almost-demonic grin rises at the corners of his mouth, and suddenly he's not Tyler Walker anymore. He's something else entirely. A demi-god in all his power and an animal in all its savagery.

His fingers are gone from both my pussy and my hair as he sits back on his haunches and delivers his first words so low I barely hear them.

"Get on all fours." I'm so surprised by his change in demeanor that my body reacts instinctively and my curiosity is begging to speed this all up.

"Spread your legs wide and show me your wet little cunt." Here's the thing. Dirty talk is my weakness. The assertive way a man tells me what to do, how to do it, and when to do it has always had a direct link to my clit.

I do as he asks. After all, we have a deal and I always keep my promises.

With one hand splayed across the space between my shoulder blades, he pushes down until my cheek presses against the sheets. I've never been happier to have a high thread count. I need my skin to be in an impeccable state to charge the rates I do.

"If you could see yourself now. Dripping wet, your pussy lips open and ready to take my cock." My inner walls clench with the mental image he's offering me.

"You're wasting time, Tyler. At this rate, you're going to lose your bet." With a *tsk*, he rises from the bed and heads to the chair where his slacks are neatly folded. He's out of my sight, but from the sound of it all, I'm guessing lube and condoms are firmly in his hands and I'm about to get fucked to within an inch of my sanity.

The bed dips but no words are exchanged, we're beyond the formalities. One big, strong hand is on my right ass cheek, his thumb sliding from my coccyx down to my puckered hole. He doesn't linger there but slides down to my pussy and pushes his thumb inside just long enough to make me squirm with pleasure.

I'm not telling him that, though. Time's a-wasting and I can almost taste the bitterness of my cash-out. Before I can even finish that thought in my head, his cock is plunging inside me. I was so fixated on the money I'm hoping to make, I didn't even hear him slide the condom on. I know he did though, because safety was our number one concern in our contract. Being tested regularly is non-negotiable—proof of results in-hand, along with the use of condoms. Always. I do *not* want to be getting myself knocked up with a basic stranger's baby. No thank you.

I grunt with the force of his thrust. It's the slap across my flesh that brings me back to the moment without fail. I wasn't expecting it but I am now.

"Stay with me, Rose. You don't get to wander off into your head." Fuck, for someone who barely knows me, he can read my body language like a pro.

I don't speak, it's not what this is. This is his show, his game. His release. Though my pleasure seems to be his number one priority.

After stilling inside me for a couple of seconds, my body adjusting to his size, he slides out slowly before reaching down and grabbing the longer hair on the top of my head. With a sharp pull, I'm now in an awkward position and it turns me the fuck on.

It's almost demeaning, but it's not. I'm at his mercy, and the pleasure courses through my body as I try to hold my position.

He slams back into me and I swear to fuck, I can feel him in my throat. I swallow hard, making sure his dick isn't there, as ridiculous as it may be.

"I love that you doubted me, Rose. But your body? It's a fucking work of art and I'm the goddamn maestro about to give it the final touch."

From that moment, he plants a hand on my hip and fucks me like I'm weightless, hitting my g-spot like his cock has a fucking GPS on the broad head.

Every time he bottoms out, I groan. My body lights up with electric sparks that begin at the base of my spine and erupt all through my nerve endings.

I'm close. I can't fucking believe how close I am, and that motherfucker knows it. I can hear it in his voice when he tells me to take it. To take *him*.

I forget where I am. Who I am. All I know is the pleasure that I'm feeling, the intensity of his touch, the utter delight of his dick pounding my pussy over and over again.

A voice is crying out "more" and "harder" and it's not until I feel the rawness in my throat that I realize it's me. I'm begging for him to lose all of his precious control.

And he does. He's like a fucking tsunami pummeling me like the waves against the shore. His power is without hold. He's lost to the lust and I'm loving every single minute of it.

"Yes! Oh my God, yes!" My throat aches from the position but I love that he's controlling my posture, my everything. I can't move unless he's the one granting it, and I never knew I had a sub kink, but here we are.

"You ready to come, Sweet Rose?" I don't answer, letting my body do all the talking instead as I put my weight against my palms and push my hips back until he's impossibly deeper.

I get another slap for that move. Taking away his control is apparently a no-no for Mr. Billionaire.

"Behave," is the only word he growls out before I feel the silky touch of warm lube running down the crack of my ass.

Anticipation is half the pleasure. Knowing he's going to breach my ass but not knowing if it's with his fingers or his cock. Either will do, to be honest. At this point, I'm a fucking mess and he could fist fuck me and I probably wouldn't mind it.

Two fingers.

That's what I get just as his dick pummels that deep ache inside my pussy.

I lose it. The anticipation, the game, the sheer feel of him and his precise thrusts are too much for my body and mind to resist.

Goodbye, extra money.

The shit we allow for a good fucking orgasm.

I gasp right before I scream out his name, my pussy pulsing, my walls squeezing his cock like it's begging for it to stay and never leave.

"Jesus fucking Christ!" He punctuates every word with a thrust that sends me reeling even harder than I thought possible.

And then he's gone and I'm suddenly on my back, legs spread, pussy open like a fucking gift to the gods. His mouth is on me, his tongue licking up every single drop of cum I give him. Because that's what I'm doing, giving him my orgasm, and he's lapping it up like a treasure he intends to keep safe.

I'm only remotely aware that he's jacking himself off as he eats my pussy from back to front—sucking on my clit with every pass—sucking on my lips as my orgasm comes down and my breathing returns to something close to normal.

My eyes open just in time to watch him rise on his haunches, look me straight in the eyes, and stroke himself to climax. His dick pointing to my opening, streams of cum landing on my mound, my belly button, my tits, until there's nothing left.

Our eyes meet and a slow grin adorns his beautifully plump lips, coated with my juices, before he announces. "Fourteen minutes and twenty-six seconds."

Fucker.

He's lucky the orgasm was definitely worth it.

Needless to say, light sleepers or not, we both pass out after a quick hot shower and don't open our eyes until the sun bursts through the sheer curtains, the breeze a welcome interruption to a dreamless night.

It only takes my brain a few seconds to remember the text from last night and my body tenses all over again.

I'm guessing I'll need to take another trip to Staten Island soon.

# CHAPTER FIVE
## RIVER

An in-room massage is my new favorite thing. I've got the day to myself in a luxury hotel, so here I am, getting any and all kinks out of my back. Tyler organized it for me as he dressed for meetings with his clients today. The way that man puts on a suit is almost as toe curling as when he takes it off.

"How's the pressure for you?"

The masseuse pulls me from my thoughts. I hate it when they do that. It ruins my whole relaxation mode and pulls me into the present.

"Fine, thank you." I might hate talking during a massage, but I don't want her to stop whatever she's doing with those magic hands, so I keep my voice sweet.

The tranquil flute sounds coming from the speakers, combined with the sweet almond oil smell, do their job in helping me relax again. The lines have been blurred a little too far this weekend with Tyler, and I can't allow that to continue. No matter how good that orgasm was. I need to remind myself that he's nothing more than a client.

The one thing I've been avoiding drifts back into my thoughts. The text message. It was only five words, but those five words could ruin everything I've worked so hard to build and keep separated. My worlds were never meant to collide, and now I'm going to have to face it head on. With one person I hoped would never know.

Will he look at me differently? Will he still respect me?

As much as I hate to ask myself that question—I know I have nothing to be ashamed of—I'm not blind to the judgment that comes with what I do.

Is he one of those people?

Fuck! This isn't a road I want to go down right now, I'll deal with it on Monday. Tyler is paying for my time, and anything less than my full attention is unprofessional. I need to put River in a box and keep Rose in the forefront; the most confident woman in every room.

"Mrs. Walker...? Mrs. Walker, I'm all done now." I must've fallen asleep. That sixty minutes went by faster than I'd like.

"Thank you." My words are muffled as I try to lift my heavy head. I'd forgotten Tyler checked us in as Mr. and

Mrs. at the hotel. Just another stark reminder that this is all fake.

"No problem, Mrs. Walker. Don't forget to hydrate plenty, and enjoy the rest of your stay. I'll get someone to come back for the bed later so you can just get up when you're ready."

The room door clicks open and doesn't close again. I wait... and wait... and hear a shuffle.

"Hello?" I lift my head fully, pushing up onto my elbows so I can see the entrance.

"Enjoy yourself?" Leaning casually against the doorframe, Tyler's tight smile is accompanied with a raised eyebrow.

A sleepy nod is my response—the well-practiced, seductive and demure kind. He's tense, and as much as he's trying to hide it, I can see it in his posture. After a morning of undoubtedly stressful meetings, I know what he needs.

Sliding off the massage table, I let the towel that was around my waist drop to the floor, leaving me bare to him. His eyes drink me in, giving me a powerful sense of control, like I hold all the answers to his troubles. He pushes off the door, closing it behind him as he prowls toward me.

I drop to my knees—my intentions clear as I unzip his suit pants. His cock is straining to be released, so I do just that. Palming his balls in one hand, I lick from the base of his shaft all the way up to the tip, flicking my tongue over the cum-leaking slit. My lips envelop the broad head, sucking like it's giving me life until I hear the deep tremble of his guttural groan. The sound spurs me on, the fact that I'm taking even an iota of his control actually makes me wet for him.

To say I'm surprised is an understatement. For the second time in as many days, I don't need to lube up. My mouth slides down the length of his cock until my nose is pressed against his groin. With my tongue flattened against the hard, velvety surface of his cock, I add and relent the pressure without a set rhythm. There's nothing more fun than keeping them guessing.

It doesn't take long for the head of his dick to hit the back of my throat, the tangy taste of him hitting my tongue before practically ramming my tonsils. He's close, I can feel it. My suspicion is confirmed as his hand clutches the crown of my head and his hips thrust forward, making me gag around him. Saliva drips from the corners of my mouth as he takes control of the situation, fucking my face with a deep, primal need.

Rolling his balls in one hand and digging my nails into his ass with the other, I let him slam in and out of my mouth, making sure to look him straight in the eyes as he takes exactly what he needs. What he's paid for. Tyler's grunts speed up, his groans in perfect rhythm with each plunge of his cock inside my eagerly awaiting mouth.

"Fuck!"

One... two... three sharp thrusts, and he stills as warm streams of salty cum shoot down the back of my throat. I continue to suck his cock like a popsicle, concentrating on the tip until every last drop is gone.

Grabbing both sides of my head, he pulls me up to his face and kisses me so intensely I almost forget where I am. It's disconcerting, the filthy tenderness of his lips on mine, but my mask is firmly on and my emotions completely off.

"I wish I could repay the favor, Rose." He rests his forehead against mine. "But I only came back to make sure you had everything you needed before tonight." Pulling his head away again, his hands still on the sides of my face, he looks at me, really looks at me. "Fuck, you're beautiful."

"You know you could've sent me a text or called?" I let a smile play on my lips, not allowing him to see how much his behavior is unnerving me.

"Yeah, I know." He runs his hands through his short dark hair, resting them at the back of his neck and looking to the ceiling. "I also just wanted to see you."

This is new. He's never done this before. I don't know what's changed on this trip, but does he...?

No.

He can't.

I'm reading too much into this. The text message is still fucking with me and my Rose mask has slid off one too many times this weekend.

"Well, now you've seen me, you should get back to your meetings and allow me to get ready for tonight." Flashing him my best seductive smile, I steel my spine for my next words. "Time to show your bitchy ex-wife that she made a huge..." I pause to eye his crotch for emphasis. "Mistake."

His own smile falters slightly before transforming back into Tyler—the business man—again. He's letting his own façade slip far too much this weekend as well.

"Right, yes. Exactly that. I'll leave you to do whatever you need to do. Oh, and Rose?" He's already started to walk back toward the door, leaving me naked in the middle of the room.

"Yes?"

"The dress is in the closet, and there's a necklace in the top drawer of my bedside table I'd like you to wear."

He's out the door before I can even respond. Probably for the best. That whole conversation was fueled by something we've never had between us in the past. I need to remind myself that I'm Rose this weekend. *Rose*. Not River. River can't give Tyler what he needs or wants. Well, neither can Rose, but at least Rose is good for a temporary fix.

Which is all this is.

A temporary fix.

Okay, so I've changed my mind. Room service might be my new favorite thing. I indulged in a few items from the lunch menu before spending a good couple of hours in the deep bath full of steaming water and jasmine scented bubbles. One good thing about wearing a wig; I don't have to worry about styling my hair after the bath.

The dress Tyler chose for me is nothing less than exquisite. It's a beautiful teal-green, floor-length, mermaid-style gown. Ruching at the front makes my chest look awesome, and the back comes so low it just skims my ass crack. The thin straps are the only thing holding it in place. It's times like this, I'm thankful for my shapely hips. There's no denying I fill this dress out beautifully. The silk feels like satin waterfalls against my skin, and I can't help admiring the slight shimmer as I catch my reflection in the floor-length mirror.

Making sure my wig is in place—styled half up-half down, with a few loose curls around my face—I head for the drawer, curious about the necklace. For a guy, Tyler has great taste in jewelry.

"Holy shit!" This thing clearly looks like a copy of the necklace from Titanic, and I can't help quoting the first thing that comes to mind upon seeing it. "But I thought the old lady dropped it into the ocean in the end."

"Well, baby, I went down and got it for ya." Tyler's voice makes me jump, and I squeak when the box almost falls from my grip.

"Did you just quote a Britney Spears video?" I don't know what shocks me the most, the sheer size of the necklace, or the fact that he can quote a cheesy line from a pop diva's music video.

A sheepish, almost boyish, look crosses his handsome face. "It was my sister's favorite song."

Something inside me melts the tiniest bit, but just as I'm about to ask for more information, he transforms back into his signature broody billionaire persona. That window is now firmly closed, leaving me more than a little curious.

"Are you ready?" It's now that I actually see him properly, taking in what he's wearing, and oh holy mother of all fucks.

Wow.

Tyler looks fucking hot as sin in his black Tom Ford tuxedo.

"I am. Just about to put this piece of art on. Thank you, by the way. It's beautiful."

He walks over to me and holds his hand out to help me stand, gently turning me so my back is to him as I pass him the necklace.

"It's nowhere near as beautiful as the woman wearing it tonight." The words are whispered into my ear as he slowly puts the necklace around my neck, taking his time to stroke his fingers over my skin as he moves my hair aside and closes the clasp.

It sends tingles throughout my body, but the sweetness of it all is almost too much to handle.

I'm spared replying as Business Tyler takes over again. "Come on then, we can't be late. I need to be the first one there to greet everyone as they arrive."

Nodding, I grab my small silver bag and slip on my silver Louboutins. I swear, they have a shoe for every occasion. We leave the room arm in arm and head to the lobby, where we're shown out to the gardens. A giant canopy and the sides of the winding path are both covered in sparkling fairy lights. My breath catches as Tyler leads the way. At the entrance, we're greeted with champagne from a server, one arm outstretched in a gesture for us to enter the glamorous outdoor tent.

The entire setting is bathed in elegance. A crystal chandelier hangs from the slightly pointed center, and round tables surround a temporary dance floor for after-dinner dancing. I glance at the movement to our right and realize they've planned for a live band—the three men and one woman quietly setting up as we make our way across the empty space.

I'm obviously too busy taking it all in as I feel Tyler tense beside me. It draws me back to the present and I notice someone I was really hoping to avoid for a little longer. The ex-wife.

"What the fuck is she even doing here?" Tyler mumbles so only I can hear. He wanted to be the first to arrive. This wasn't part of his plan, and the bitch knew it. She knows what he likes, she was with him long enough to know he has rituals. He likes to check the place out and make sure it's how he wants it before his guests start arriving, so he can greet them properly as they do.

This is going to throw off his whole night. So much for a non sex-filled weekend. Tyler is going to need to get this out of his system later. Not that I'm complaining. After all, I'm not opposed to having orgasms.

His grip tightens on my hip as his entire body trembles with pent up anger. Throwing my shoulders back, I turn to face him—one palm on his cheek, my voice low and steady.

"Look at me." It takes a second, but his eyes meet my gaze, the control he so desperately craves slipping slightly. "You are not her little bitch. Do you hear me? You do not react to her tantrums and when we get back to the hotel, I'll let you fuck my ass."

My words crease the corners of his eyes, the stress alleviating slightly. I guess the idea of sinking his cock into my ass makes him feel more in control.

I turn back to stand beside Tyler, ever the doting girlfriend, presenting ourselves as one unit. It's then that Brett and Cora notice we've arrived and approach us, traitorous smiles plastered on their faces.

"He's just as bad." He speaks quietly through gritted teeth, just before gracing them both with his well-rehearsed business smile. "Brett, Cora, I see you're both here already. Our guests will be arriving soon. Did you check to see if everything was to your liking?" He's asking out of politeness, but he's still going to check it all out himself. There's no way he leaves the finer details to anyone else, especially not this pair of dicks.

To be honest, I'm impressed with how he's handling this. In his shoes, I would have already acted out my most lethal revenge.

"All a-okay, bro."

Tyler's hand flinches when Brett calls him bro. From what I've gathered, they grew up together and have always been really close. I don't know what happened for Brett to sleep with his best friend and business partner's wife, but that shit is definitely not brotherly.

"Come on, we'll leave the women to go powder their noses. I'll show you some of the changes I've made." Brett stands, and Tyler bristles. I squeeze his hand and rub some slow circles into his palm, subtly letting him know he's got this.

"You good with that, Rose?" If I was one of his clients, he wouldn't be asking me that. He'd just agree and go on ahead.

I can handle myself well in most situations—it's a practiced art—so it's all part of the package. Asking for my permission now has nothing to do with my feelings and everything to do with the uncomfortable situation that is Cora fucking Walker. No one can know who I am and what I do which, for anyone else, being alone with his ex-wife could be a complication. After all, she knows him best.

Or so she thinks.

Long-term jobs like this one demand hardcore homework for us both. I have a cover story for them to learn and I must know everything about their habits, their lives, their personal situations.

Let's just say, I'm damn good at my job.

Turning to face him, I run a hand down his cheek, sliding the other up his arm to rest behind his head. "You know I am, handsome."

Relief washes over his face as I pull his head to mine, capturing his lips in a passionate, all-consuming kiss. His arms wrap around me, resting just above my ass as I hear a nasally mumble from behind me, followed by a low "shh."

Ignoring them, I continue nipping at Tyler's bottom lip, before gently sucking on his tongue and pulling away.

"Thank you." Tyler winks and kisses the top of my head, before patting my ass and walking over with Brett to the nervous looking Hotel manager standing by the bar area.

Taking a deep breath, I steel myself for what I know is going to be an onslaught of pure bitch, before plastering on my own fake smile and taking a seat beside the ex.

"I'm sure that wasn't necessary." Her sneer actually makes me laugh a little inside. I love that she's this jealous, as that was exactly my intention.

"Oh, I know, it's mortifying." I lower my head slightly, feigning embarrassment, when really, I'm just trying to hide the smirk I can't control. "We just... you know how it is when you're in the honeymoon period. You just can't keep your hands off each other." I accidently let a giggle slip, but it has the desired effect and works with the attitude I'm trying to portray.

"Yeah, well it won't last for long. Why do you think I jumped ship? He's not all he says he is, you know." She's acting like she knows things I don't, secrets that could break me when really, it's none of my fucking business.

My shrug clearly isn't the response she wanted.

"I don't trust you. And I won't stop until I find something to ruin you. So you better watch out."

Woah, where did that come from? I've been perfectly pleasant to the psycho cunt, and she hits me with this shit?

"Look…" I lose the innocent shy girl attitude I've been giving her. "I don't know where this animosity is coming from. You cheated on him, *with his best fucking friend.* You didn't want him any more. You have no right to interfere in the here and now, so keep your plastic fucking nose out of other people's business."

The shock on her face is evident—wide eyes and flaring nostrils—she didn't expect me to bite back.

Interesting.

She's clearly just testing the waters, seeing what she can get away with, and it isn't a fucking lot. While I'm working, my clients are a priority. But if she thinks she can threaten me like that, she's lost her goddamn mind.

Also, she's pissed me the fuck off.

*Deep breaths, River.*

Before anything else is said, Cora stands from her chair, nose in the air, and heads toward the guys, draping herself over Brett as they talk with the manager.

Well, I guess she's done talking then.

Finally able to relax, I sit back and take my time admiring the room. It really is stunning. The fairy light theme has continued inside as well as out, and I love it. Some are gently twinkling, making it look like the night sky against the black cloth of the canopy.

My small bag vibrates twice against my hip, the chain over my shoulder keeping it in place. Two vibrations means it's a message on my personal phone. Do I really want to look at it right now?

I'm not one for shoving my head in the sand, so yeah, I'm looking. But if it's him, he can wait until I'm home before I reply. I just don't have the brain capacity to deal with that over the phone. A face-to-face conversation is needed.

**Unknown:** Watch your back, whore.

It's not him.

# Chapter Six

## River

With the weekend over and my wallet thicker, I put on my bad bitch panties and spend the mandatory twenty-five minutes on the ferry to Staten Island.

Any respectable Manhattanite knows that too much time spent in the suburbs kicks that biological clock into working mode. Personally, I just don't like the quiet, somewhat peaceful, life of the Forgotten Borough—their nickname, not mine. The last nine years have been pretty chaotic, and I guess I'm just used to the hustle and bustle of the busy city streets.

My short hair whips left and right with the wind as I watch the space between me and the Financial District grow wider with every minute. I love living here. The constant murmur of life reassures me, a welcomed companion on nights where all I have is my Netflix queue. My building is small and recently renovated to conform to city regulations. Though rats and leaky ceilings are typically frowned upon, they're not impossible to find, either.

Everest never liked living in the city. To be honest, I'm surprised they settled down in Staten Island. I thought maybe they'd buy a little house somewhere at the foot of the Appalachian Mountains or on the coast so they could meditate and do yoga on the beach. I suspect it has something to do with me, and not wanting to wander off too far. Kai lives over here as well, so that helps.

*Kai.*

*Fuck.*

We've known each other for the better part of our lives, which means I can practically anticipate every one of his moves. I know everything about him; his passions and his turn-offs, I know his recycled jokes that I can imagine him using on his kids one day. Fucking dad jokes. He's not even thirty yet, and sometimes sounds like he's fifty and trying to sound cool with his teenage sons.

This conversation is going to be hard. He'll be shocked, pissed even, and maybe a little disappointed, but when the shock wears off, he'll come around and we'll have an adult conversation about my life choices. Then we'll either fuck, or drink ourselves into a stupor and then fuck. I imagine he'll come up with a dozen reasons why I shouldn't be doing this job, and then another dozen solutions so I can stop.

Kai is a fixer and there's no doubt in my mind that he'll try to "fix" this. Fix *me*.

That's the crux of the problem right there. I don't need to be fixed. I don't need to be saved or swept away. I'm doing what needs to be done to take care of my family, and Everest—bless his free-loving heart—is my only blood.

I turn at the sound of laughter and smile at the little boy blowing bubbles into the salty air. Every time one pops, he belts out a laugh so free and real it makes my heart squeeze. His mother is laughing with him but she's not looking at the bubbles, she's looking at him. She's watching and waiting for that majestic sound to erupt from his mouth. Like she lives for it. Like she's teetering at the edge of a cliff and his happiness is the only reason she doesn't fall off. The bags under her tired eyes are put in sharp relief by the harsh sun, her clothes are simple and tattered at the edge of her sleeves. Her hair is up in a messy bun, and not the kind you get from a tutorial on TikTok. The real kind. The bun that you definitely did not work fifteen minutes on to give you a certain type of look.

Despite all of these things, this woman is smiling and laughing with her son like everything in life is perfect. And for her, it probably is, and I can appreciate the joy in it.

I wonder what she thinks of me? If she's even noticed me. With my Prada brushed-leather and nylon boots, Fendi knee-length coat, and a carefully applied face of make-up, I may look like I've got my shit together... if only she knew. The outfit is my armor, which I definitely need today.

Turning back to the view of Manhattan getting farther and farther away, I close my eyes and think. What *do* I wish for? If a genie were to swoop down onto this ferry and give me three wishes, what would they be?

Fixing my gaze on the horizon, I look at nothing in particular. Instead, I'm rummaging through my mind's eye, searching for a time in my life when shit was simple. Where I didn't have to be the responsible one. Where I didn't have to give up my college education, or my parents' mobile home that we kept on communal land with six other families. A time where selling entrance fees to my vagina wasn't the best option. At one point, the only option.

I'd wish for money, I suppose. It's what got me into this life and would maybe get me out.

Our ferry crosses its twin, both going in opposite directions, and my gaze zeroes in on an old lady with long, gray hair flying in the wind as she looks down at the water.

What would Psyche have wished for? When she was up on that hill—alone and afraid—what had been her wish?

Love?

Probably.

Except, I had that, right? Love from my brother. From Kai, in his own way. I mean, he loves to fuck me, that's for sure. To push me up against the nearest flat surface and bury his dick deep inside me. He fucking loves that. Me? Well, after today's conversation, I'm pretty sure I'll lose a couple of brownie points.

In my hand, my personal phone vibrates and when I look down, I smile.

"Speak of the devil and his face flashes on your screen." My words go unheard as I speak to no one, but my smile disappears when I read his text message.

**Kai**: At arrivals. Waiting in my truck.

Fuck.

My first instinct is to pretend I'm not coming. Tell him I slept in. Tell him I'm not feeling well. Tell him I missed the ferry and would be on the next one. Anything other than what I finally type out as a response.

**Me**: See you in ten.

The first sign that Kai is pissed off is obvious—his scowl. Normally, his gorgeous features are blessed by the sunrays making his honey-colored eyes seem almost ethereal. Any other time, he'd flash me a hint of dimple. He'd pull me in as soon as I was within arm's reach, and gift me both dimples before slamming his mouth to mine, greeting me like we've been married for two decades. It's our thing... but it doesn't mean much, to be honest.

"You're pissed." I state the obvious just to hear the sound of my own voice.

"Get in the truck." Wow. He must be seething.

I don't argue, there's no point. We need to get this episode out of the way and get on with our lives.

I thought maybe we'd do it during the car ride. He'd ask me why. I'd tell him the truth. He'd yell something about him taking care of me and I'd tell him to go fuck himself.

Then he'd side eye me and we'd both fall into laughter. In my mind, we'd settle this whole thing by the time his truck pulled up to my brother's house.

None of that happened. Not a single fucking thing.

The entire fifteen minutes in the car was complete and total silence. No talking, no music, no open window. The only sound was the truck engine.

So here we are, parked in my brother's driveway.

I watch as Kai turns off the engine, shakes his head like he can't fathom what's happening, then opens the truck door before walking out.

I stare at him as he briskly makes his way to the front door, where Petal is smiling up at him as he crosses her threshold. Her eyes land on mine and she frowns.

I can't tell if she knows or not. I mean, why are we here if they aren't in the know?

Fucking hell. Time to face the firing squad.

With a deep breath, I slowly step out of the truck and heft my Michael Kors over my shoulder before I saunter over to Petal, placing a soft kiss on her rosy cheek.

"Hey beautiful."

"Hey gorgeous."

This kind of greeting started after Petal had taken a class on positivity and lifting women up with words. I'm okay with this because, yeah, women need to empower other women. But then, who the fuck am I to lift anyone up when the only thing I know how to rise is my legs for a harder pounding?

"What's up with Kai? Did y'all have a fight on the way here?" Okay, so at least she doesn't know.

"Nope. Found him like this at St. George, just standing in front of his truck, brooding." I flick my gaze behind her and almost wince at the death glare from the kitchen threshold. Jesus, this can't just be about me and my job.

"I have some Florida water left that I can spray in the kitchen. The lilac amethyst crystal is already there so it'll double up." She hugs me tight like she wants to rid me of all bad energy through love and invasion of private space. I used to roll my eyes at their unwavering beliefs that sage and candles could make the world a better place.

Maybe it can, what the fuck do I know? My life is anything but *sage*, and the only candles I use are for kink.

Taking my hand and squeezing once, she looks me in the eye and declares. "I saw it in a dream." Oh, for fuck's sake, what is she going to tell me now? "You and Kai. It's meant to be." This time, I do roll my eyes. I love Petal but that ship sailed a long time ago, when I saw his dick pummeling in and out of my best friend's pussy.

I mean, it's not like we were together. Hell, he didn't even know how I felt about him and thankfully, never knew that I saw them together.

"Petal, no. That's not going to happen." She doesn't have time to respond, just throws me a look that says all is going to be perfect. With a sigh, I let her lead me through the kitchen door and face the wrath that is Kai Briggs.

"Wanna beer, River? It's organic. Got it from the home brewer in West Virginia last month." Hard pass on that shit.

"No, thanks. I'll just have a glass of water." I can feel Kai's stare burning a hole in my profile but I don't dare glance at him. We haven't spoken since that text, and I swear I can feel the years of friendship and secret crushes disintegrating with every passing second we ignore the elephant in the kitchen.

"I'm so happy you wanted to see us, Kai, but I feel like we're missing something? Do you have bad news?" Petal is throwing questions at him as she sprays the kitchen down with Florida water. "Oh gods, did someone die? It would explain all this bad energy around you." With a frown, she sprays Kai's head. I don't think it's supposed to be used like that. In fact, I'm pretty sure my mother said it was only for the room, not for people.

"Yeah, I have something to say." Kai looks at me and I try to plead with my eyes, try to beg him not to do this. I'm two painful words away from getting up and running out so I don't have to see my brother's expression when Kai tells him what I do. Or the guilt he'll never be able to shake when he finds out why I do it.

Silently, I plead with my entire soul, tears brimming against my eyelashes, and I swear I feel him back off. No one else sees it, but then again, no one knows Kai the way I do. Not even Everest.

"So, out with it." Everest hands Kai a beer, the yellow and green label advertising the beer's name—"Orgbrew". It's a stupid name. Obviously, marketing wasn't their strong suit when they decided to mass produce. With a name like that, I bet it tastes like an ogre's pissfest.

Kai eyes the bottle with regret, probably wishing he hadn't said yes to the beer, before landing his anger-filled gaze on me. Or maybe it's hurt. I'm not sure, I can't tell.

"River goes by the name of Rose." My life shatters in that moment. I feel like he's just broken the last remaining piece of my heart, slicing me deep with his need to what? Protect me? Save me?

Destroy me and my family.

"Duh, that's her middle name." With his head tilted back, Everest takes a long pull from his beer, his bright green eyes, the exact color of mine, looking at me pointedly in a way that no one else can see. What does that mean? Is he...? Does he know?

A single tear escapes my eye but I wipe it down before anyone can catch sight of it. At least that's what I think until I lift my gaze to Kai, and see him watching me. It's then he makes his decision. Taking one for the team.

"Well, fuck." He shrugs, like he didn't just scare them half to death. "I thought maybe she was a double agent or some shit." I put on my Rose face and act like it's all a big misunderstanding. I have no idea if his complete one-eighty works on Everest and Petal but I don't look at them to find out. I'm still reeling from the emotional rollercoaster Kai threw me into, and as soon as we're away from curious ears, I'm going to give him a piece of my mind.

Now I'm the one pissed off, and Kai can sense it. His eyes harden again as we both gear up for a fight. *You wanted this? Let's do it.*

"Wanna go for a drive?" My protective walls go straight up, but with sugar in my voice I tell him I'd love to.

Petal sighs audibly, like her dreams just came true. Her literal dreams from last night, apparently.

We pull up at Allison Pond Park and he doesn't have to tell me where we're headed, I already know. It was our quiet spot growing up, the peaceful sounds of nature and the rush of water falling from the fountain was perfect for teenage secrets and romantic fantasies.

It's where I first told him I hated living like a vagabond. That I wanted to have a house and my own room. And a dog that didn't belong to an entire community.

It's where he first told me that he'd lost his virginity to Freya fucking Murphy. Except, it wasn't a secret to me, but there was no fucking way I would ever tell him that. So, I just smiled and said, "Congrats." Inside, though? I fell apart all over again.

It's ironic that we would have this conversation here because, looking back, this is the first place I put on my Rose mask. The first time I walled up to avoid collapsing on myself.

"Funny story." These are the first two words he says to me since asking if I wanted to go for a drive. I highly doubt anything about his conversation is going to be funny. I don't say that though. The stage is all his.

"I have a buddy at the site, nice guy but a bit of an asshole with women. And he says to me, 'Hey, Kai, is your girl a redhead now?'" My brain is scrambling, taking inventory of all the places I could have possibly run into a construction worker from Staten Island. The only time I ever wear that wig is with Tyler, and there's no way a blue-collar worker could pay for even an appetizer in the places we've been.

"I laugh out loud and tell him I've never seen you as a redhead."

My brain does an immediate freeze and then goes into reverse.

"*Your* girl?" I emphasize the word "your" and those are my first words to him. "You've probably fucked half of Staten Island and maybe a good ten percent of Manhattan, and when he says "your" girl you think of...?" I let my phrase die out because how is that even logical?

"Don't be ridiculous, River. I don't sleep around and you know it. Hell, the last time I fucked it was you." He's right, he doesn't sleep around but I tend to get bitchy when I feel cornered. I wish he did though just so I could hate him and be done with him.

I'm such a fucking hypocrite.

"You, on the other hand..." Fuck. Here we go.

I turn to face the fountain, my arms crossed and leaning on the steel banister.

"Just get to the point, Kai. I'm tired and want to go home." I'm ready for this to be over. Fuck, I don't think I'm ready at all but, come on, surely the anticipation and the waiting game is more painful than the actual ripping of the Band-Aid.

God, I hope this doesn't spell out the end of us. I'm definitely not ready for that.

"He showed me the picture on Page Six. Your face was clear as day, but your hair... It was all wrong. I thought, no, it can't be her. But then I looked at the rest of the picture and, River? I can recognize the slope of your neck anywhere. The way it dips at the foot of your throat." He places a finger on my neck and a thousand goosebumps erupt, my skin on fire. Then he retraces his path and before he says a word, I just know what he's going to tell me.

He stops at the side of my neck and circles the heart shaped beauty mark that lies there, innocently.

"I saw *this* and I knew." Kai sighs, letting his hand drop then turning to mirror my position. "When were you going to tell me you're seriously dating some rich asshole?" The hurt in his voice is like a cold shower to my heart. Closing my eyes, I send a thousand prayers of thanks to the sky and slip on my mask. I can handle this a lot better than him knowing I fuck for a price. It's not an easy feat, making peace with a job like mine, but I've managed. The guilt is just a long-ago memory at this point. What I cannot—*will* not—accept are looks of disappointment and disgust on the faces of those I love the most. The only people in my life that mean a damn to me.

"I didn't want to hurt you." My voice is thick, my heartbeat like a subway speeding through an empty station. "I was going to tell you all but I knew you'd disapprove." How easily the lies flow.

"It's not my place to disapprove, Riv. I'm not your keeper but yeah, I can't say it didn't hurt. I wish you'd told me, you know?" He clears his throat and turns, leaning on the banister, his thick arms crossed over his chest. A family walks by, three kids running ahead of the parents while the father pushes an empty stroller. We let them pass before continuing our conversation.

"I thought we could start something serious. You know, now that we're settled." I almost laugh at his boyish voice edged with a hint of hardness.

Shaking my head in disbelief, I turn to the side so I can look at the beauty that is his profile. Strong, straight nose, hard jaw with enough stubble to leave a mark on my thighs when he eats my pussy like a savage.

The thought makes me wet and like a hound, he snaps his head my way, his eyes squinting like he can smell my arousal. "Did you think I wouldn't find out? That you could change your name and have your high rolling fun with New York's *hottest* bachelor, then come home and slum it with me?" So, not a pussy hound, then.

"Don't be ridiculous." I throw his words back at him. "He asked me out, I said yes. End of." Technically, it's the truth. "And Rose goes well with the red hair."

He snorts his distaste. "Why the wig?" He can't even look at me right now.

"You know what they say, redheads have more fun." I try to lighten the situation but all I do is piss him off.

"No, they don't say that. Stop fucking around, River, and tell me what the fuck is going on!" He's practically yelling, the family vibe dying with every "fuck" he throws into the air.

"Shh, there are kids out here," I whisper-yell at him, mortified that two of the three kids are looking at us with gaping mouths. Great, we'll forever be the couple who cussed at the park, in their story.

"Dammit." This time his curse is barely audible. Kai is a family man at heart. Right now, he's kicking himself for being a bad example to those kids. I wish I were the family type but alas, I'm just the side piece.

"So, that's it? You're dating Tyler Walker, the soulless mogul?" His words are practically sneered and the insult gnaws at my conscience. "Does he even know your real name?"

"He's not soulless, Kai. Don't be a judgmental asshole. And what does it matter? Rose *is* my real name. Albeit my middle one." Avoiding eye contact, I center my gaze on his neck. Bad idea, because as I watch his Adam's apple slowly bob up and down, I want to wash my lying mouth out with soap then lick him all over.

"So is he the reason you just shut down my texts when I'm trying to look out for you?"

"That's insulting, Kai. I have my own mind. You know me well enough to know I handle my own shit."

"Whatever, River. You do you. Come on, I'll drive you back to Everest's." Now I'm the one who's angry. How dare he take this holier than thou attitude like he's the one who baptized baby Jesus, and now he can pass judgement on who I do or don't fuck? How fucking dare he?

In my head, I mimic his *whatever,* and in the privacy of my own thoughts I also flip him off with both middle fingers.

"No. Just take me back to the ferry. I've had enough of peace and love for one day." I walk away and leave him there, knowing he'll follow in no time.

With every step, I truly believe there's no going back. He's hurt. It's new for him.

I've been hurt for years so I know what I'm talking about.

It took a while, but here we are.

Over and done.

# Chapter Seven

## River

After Kai dropped me off at the ferry last week, I spiraled a little. For the first time since I've been doing this, my personal life clashed with Rose. Luckily, the shit didn't hit the fan too much, and I know Kai will get over this—eventually. He still hasn't responded to the text I sent him a few days ago, but I'm not worrying about that. This is Kai. Once he's had time to lick his imaginary wounds, I'm sure we'll fuck and make up.

"Oh, shit!" I'm startled into actually paying attention to what I'm doing in the grocery store, bumping into something solid. Something solid that smells divine—a little like a forest after a rainfall.

"Woah, are you okay?" The deep voice pulls my gaze upward, meeting a pair of crystal blue eyes staring at me with worry.

It's him. Candy Aisle Guy.

"Oh, yeah. I'm so sorry. I wasn't paying attention an—"

"Don't worry about it, let me help you with that."

I hadn't even realized I dropped anything. Fuck, this guy sends my brain up dick's creek without a condom.

Before I reply, he's kneeling down and picking up the whipped cream cans that fell out of my basket. There's just something about a man on his knees that does things to me. So much so, I need to suppress a shiver running down my spine straight to my clit.

"Thank you. I really appreciate it." My face is flushing as he places the cans and a box of tampons I hadn't noticed back in my basket.

"No problem. You were in your own little world. You sure you're okay?" The way he looks at me is a mix of concern and curiosity, which is unusual. I'm not used to men looking at me with anything other than lust, or more recently, disappointment.

"I'm fine, thank you, and again, I'm so sorry."

It's hard, but I finally force myself to look away from his captivating blues as I start to walk toward the counter. No big deal, I have everything I need anyway.

"Wait up!" Now *he* looks uncomfortable. Shit, did I hurt him? Is he about to ask for some kind of compensation? "I'm er... about to grab a coffee if you wanna join me..."

Well, that's a plot twist, and completely unexpected. Fireflies erupt in my belly at the thought of spending actual time with Candy Aisle Guy. I should get his real name at some point. But do I want that? Is that the smart move? I have enough going on in my life without finding out my secret crush is a big old disappointment, just like the rest of them. I have my own story about his life made up in my head, and in it... he's married. Which is why he's my safe, guilty pleasure; nothing could ever happen between us. He's just pretty to look at. Though, in my defense, the married part of my story for him is obvious from the wedding ring on his finger.

"Too soon? I mean, I can let you think about it and ask again next time?" He's looking at me with amusement now as I have an internal debate over whether or not I should have a coffee with a hot guy. *Pull yourself together, River.* I'm sure he wouldn't be asking if he was still married, would he?

"Erm..." I nod subtly down to his ring finger. "What would your wife think about that?" Awkward doesn't even begin to describe this conversation.

A shadow briefly passes through his eyes, bringing with it a kind of sadness, which dampens the mood. I feel bad about asking, but I can't go out with a guy knowing he's married. I may be an escort, but in my real life, I'm not that girl.

He clears his throat before speaking, his eyes shifting right then left before pinning me with a deep blue stare that briefly paralyzes me. "She died. So, er, no." If I thought it was awkward before, then right now is downright unbearable. Like an idiot, I search the ground for the biggest hole to whisk me away from this conversation.

"I'm sorry... for... you know, your loss?" Ground, swallow me now.

"Yeah, thanks."

And then there was silence. Like, complete and utter nothingness as we stare at each other, trying to figure out what to say next. I mean, how do you follow up with *my condolences*?

Shifting my feet, I take a deep breath and say *fuck it* inside my head.

"Okay, then, coffee sounds great. Under one condition." I give him a bright smile that probably screams psychopath, but in for a penny and all that.

"What's that?" Damn, even with his brows pinched and a look of utter confusion, he's still hot as fuck.

"You tell me your name so I don't have to keep calling you Candy Aisle Guy in my head."

"Candy Aisle Guy, huh? As opposed to Gas Station Guy?" Oh, he thinks he's funny.

"Well, yes. And Coffee Shop Guy, but I've given up on him. I don't think he's legal."

His answer is a smile so big, bright, and God damn sexy that I'm pretty sure I just wet my panties. But he doesn't stop there. Leaning in, his voice like sex and dark chocolate, he whispers in my ear. "Nathaniel Reed."

Fucking hell, now I know my panties are wet. Dripping, in fact.

"Okay, so, I am going to pay for my shopping?" My cheeks are on fire, I need to pull myself together and find some of my Rose confidence.

"And I'll meet you outside when you're done?" *Two questions, River. Really? Two questions?*

I clear my throat and throw my shoulders back, before nodding once and heading straight to the cash register.

"*Ciao*, Francesca. This is everything for today, *grazie*." At the counter, I hand over my small basket of goodies so she can ring them up, smiling like a goon as she wags her eyebrows at me. Francesca knows about everything that goes on in this store.

"I say nothing, *bella*. Be safe, and have fun. Tell me everything next time, eh?" She grins at me, knowing full well I won't tell her *everything,* but still eager for information.

"*Si*, of course, you know I will." Gossip is this woman's life-blood. Obviously I don't go around talking about my life, so I get why she's so excited. Maybe I'll give her the cliff-notes next time I'm in, just to make her happy.

"*Buono, buono. A Presto*, River."

"Yup, see you soon, Francesca." Shaking my head a little, my face actually hurting from the huge smile, I gather my things and head outside to wait for Nathaniel. *Fuck, I love his name.*

"Ready to go?"

I startle at the deep timbre of his voice, and when I turn around, I swear the color of his eyes intensifies in the bright sunlight.

"I am. Do you have somewhere in mind?"

I'm treading in unknown waters right now. Dates and one-on-one time with men while I'm 'off duty' is not something I do very often, if at all. He looks as nervous as I feel though, so I'm not uncomfortable. I mean, we've already gone through some awkward-ass shit, so I think we're good for now. If anything, I feel good about this, about doing something normal. After all this time basically stalking the guy—yeah, I'll admit to coinciding my shopping visits with his in hopes of stolen glimpses and polite smiles—and now I'm actually going for coffee with him. Okay, so it's not a date-date, but it's something.

With Kai being an ass at the moment, this comes as a welcome distraction.

"There's a place just down the stre—"

Aqua's *Barbie Girl* starts blasting from my back pocket. That's my work phone, and that ring tone means only one person.

Polly—I know that's not her real name—my old Madam. The woman who introduced me to my first client. It's unusual for her to call mid-week, which means I really should answer it. She'll only keep calling back until I do.

*Fuck's sake*, just when I'm about to do something that resembles normality.

"Sorry about this, I really should answer it." Smiling apologetically, I pull my cell from my jeans. "Hey Polly. I'm with someone right now, can I call you back?"

Nathaniel pretends he's not listening. It's hard not to when I'm standing right here. I would do the same.

"Of course, darling. Five minutes okay?" Pushy as ever, that woman. But she's done a lot for me and I owe her a few favors.

"Great, speak to you in five." I don't bother with pleasantries, she's hung up before I can say another word anyway. Efficiency is the name of the game.

"Gotta go?" Nathaniel asks, a hint of disappointment passing across his features, quickly masked with a fake smile I know all too well. I wear one often.

"Yeah. I'm sorry. I feel like I keep saying that to you today. Can we raincheck?" Putting on my best apology face, I give him a small smile. I'm shy all of a sudden—an unfamiliar emotion for me.

"Yeah, I get it, no problem." He looks around, and to my horror he plucks a pen out of a passing delivery guy's hand. As he apologizes, he takes my arm and writes a series of numbers across my palm. *His* number, I realize. When he's done, he hands the pen back with a thank you before bringing his blue gaze back to me. "The ball's in your court... fuck." He frowns. I'm confused, what's happening right now? "I don't know your name."

It's my turn to smile, and I do my best to dazzle him. "Well, I guess that's a conversation for next time."

Without giving myself a chance to think about it, I rise to my tiptoes and place a soft kiss at the corner of his mouth. Then I swiftly turn and walk away like the dramatic bitch I am.

Waiting for a client to turn up is a pain in the ass, especially when they're late. It's only five minutes, but still... I hope he doesn't think he's getting a discount or over-running on his scheduled time.

Polly's phone call earlier was a big ask, taking on a client I haven't been in contact with myself is something I haven't done for years. But she was desperate, a few of her girls called in sick, meaning Polly had to find someone on short notice. With no back-ups of her own to fill the spot, I was her best bet.

Three-thousand dollars for an hour's work was hard to resist. All I know about this guy is that he likes it rough and is into a little rope play. I gave her a hard pass on the tied-up part; I'm not okay with being vulnerable with someone I don't know. This type of play is usually done with a contract and reserved for clients I trust.

A knock on the door jolts me back to the here and now. With my Dolce & Gabbana black suede ankle strap heels, and lacy black underwear—suspenders included—I steel my spine, plaster on my Rose mask, and open the door.

*Showtime.*

"Well, hello there. Come on in." Gesturing inside, I welcome 'Rex Steele' into the small apartment. It's basically just one big bedroom, the giant 4-poster bed taking up most of the space, and a separate small bathroom in the far corner.

He's actually quite handsome, in a generic way. There's nothing that really stands out, but he's easy on the eyes. At least my job will be easier tonight. The whole money exchange thing doesn't need to happen, Polly dealt with that and will pay me when I see her in a couple of days.

After closing the door, I give my best 'come fuck me' eyes as I prowl toward him, running my hands across his chest to help him off with his shirt. As I'm undoing his top button, he grips my wrists in his hands, squeezing a little harder than necessary. This doesn't feel right, but it's three-thousand dollars and I don't want to let Polly down. *It's only for an hour.*

Rex's gaze turns from shy lust to pure ice, like he's just flipped a switch and turned off all emotions. I get the need to do that, but this isn't the way I change from River to Rose, this is something different. More sinister. I don't like it. A niggling feeling starts in my gut, the kind that keeps women like me alive.

"Rex, you're hurting me. Can you loosen your hold a little please?" The best way to deal with these guys is to avoid angering them, to keep an even tone and let them believe they're in control. After all, that's what they need.

A slow grin creeps across his face as he tightens his grip, no doubt leaving bruises at this point. It fucking hurts and need to get control of this situation.

"Rex, let go. You're hurting me." I'm struggling to pull out of his hold, finding it hard not to whimper at the increasing pain. It feels like he's cutting off the circulation to my hands, which is starting to make me panic.

His response is a low chuckle, if you can call it that. And after everything he's shown me so far, that's what scares me the most.

The way he's holding me makes it impossible to use the more subtle self-defense moves I've learned. Straight for the jugular it is then, since my legs are still free to move. I'll give him one last chance before this gets nasty.

"Rex. Please. Let. Me. Go. Now." Slow and steady. Definitely not panicking as I watch his sinister smile turn into something I wish I could erase from my brain. *Why isn't he talking?*

With my panic rising, I focus on everything I learned in Krav Maga before positioning my legs. I asked nicely. He's been warned.

The freak is just staring at his hold on my wrists, like he's fascinated with watching my hands turn whiter from lack of blood flow. I'm fucking done playing games now. With as much strength as I can, I lift my knee and hit the fucker straight in the jewels. He immediately releases his grip.

"Ah! You fucking whore!"

Finally, he speaks. Not the most original insult I've ever heard.

Not taking a moment to assess the situation, I head straight for the door. I need to get out of here and to some kind of safety.

Quickly.

I'm not fucking stupid. I don't—for one second—think I can best this guy by myself. This is the last fucking time I do a Polly a favor. Total fucking shit show.

Turning the handle to the front door, I get it partially open, only to be slammed into from behind. Panic begins to swell up from inside me again, my breaths are labored after being winded from the impact. He doesn't move, caging me in against the door, with my front pressed up to the hard surface.

"Think you're clever, do you? I'm sick of hearing your shrill little voice." His putrid breath at my ear sends bile to my throat. I may very well be in trouble right now, but fuck if I let this guy win.

He grabs onto my wig, so close to my scalp that he's actually got hold of my real hair, and yanks my head backward so I'm bent at an awkward angle. Something that tastes like ass with an awful cotton texture is shoved into my mouth, taking away any chance for me to scream. I want to try and be the strong-ass bitch that I know I am, but I'm really shitting my pants right now. Involuntary tears start forming in my eyes, running down my cheeks in a silent cry.

"Mmm, now this is what I wanted." From behind me, he licks up my tears from my chin, over my cheek, finishing just below my eye. I want to puke. "That's it, moan for me."

*My muffled cries are not for you, sick fuck.*

"You've got a little more bite than the last one. I like it. It's boring if it's too easy, you know?"

Eyes wide, tears still streaming, I struggle against his hold. I can feel every beat of my heart as it pounds heavily inside my chest. Having no idea what he's planning is probably one of the scariest things about this situation.

Kicking my foot back doesn't help me, and pain shoots through my legs as he hits the back of my thighs with something that feels like a baseball bat. My hands are free now, but I'm on the floor, the pain briefly shocking me into submission.

"Oh, you are a feisty one indeed."

The sneer on his face as I look up at him should make me cower. But there is no way in fucking hell that I'm going down without a fight. I am *not* a damsel who's going to curl up in a ball at the first sign of trouble. Pain be damned.

The back of my legs are throbbing—it's going to be hard to hide the bruises—as I try to stand. He laughs at my attempts, just fucking laughs, twirling around... wait... that's *my* fucking baseball bat! That'll teach me to keep it by the front door.

My blonde wig is discarded on the floor next to me, no doubt some of my actual hair is mixed in there too with the force it was ripped from my head.

Standing now and facing him, I slowly back up. There's a Venus de Milo sculpture by the door I can use to defend myself. Hopefully, I can grab it and do whatever I need to escape quickly. My hands are still a little numb, pins and needles making them tingle as the blood flow returns, which makes it difficult to feel around for the statue.

He's too quick, launching himself at me so fast I can barely blink. Grabbing for my wrists, he misses, and I manage to connect my fist with his face. The satisfaction of seeing blood drip from his nose is short-lived as he restrains me again.

Holding my wrists with one hand, he pulls something that looks like string from his pants pocket.

*Nah-ah... Nope... Not happening.*

My body drops like a dead weight, catching him off guard forcing him to release his grip again. I don't run for the door this time, I go straight for the window. I don't give a fuck if I've got to smash through it to get down the fire escape, I'm doing what I need to survive this crazy asshole.

On the way, I pull out the gag and scream for help at the top of my lungs. This is a busy building, someone's got to hear something. I scream and scream, and I'm so close to the window it hurts.

I don't make it.

Pain surges through me again from my scalp as he pulls me to a halt by my short hair. Something heavy connects with my skull and the corners of my vision start to turn blurry, my voice no longer making any sound as the room fades in and out... and in and out...

*Is this how I die...?*

In... and out.

A sharp scratch on my inner thigh jolts me to consciousness. My body aches all over and I don't want to open my eyes.

"Wakey wakey, my pretty little whore."

A warm breeze travels from my nipple down to my core, making me scream at the sharp sting of an open wound. Thick liquid slides down my thigh, I think it's my blood... In fact, I'm sure of it. The pain is excruciating, like a thousand salt-covered papercuts all in one place. My wrists are tied to the corners of the bed, my mouth is full of ass-flavored cotton again, and my eyes are almost swollen shut from tears.

*How long have I been unconscious?*

"Our time is almost over. You've been such a good little whore for me. Your golden skin is going to look beautiful in the new frame I bought today." The sniffing sound he exaggerates causes a chill to crawl down my spine. I refuse to give in to curiosity and open my eyes. I do not want to know.

Muffled screams fill the apartment as the sharp pain in my thigh begins again, it's like nothing I've ever felt. He's taking his time with whatever he's doing, the torture never-ending. Thrashing my body as much as I can makes it worse, and the rope burns on my wrists are now adding to the agony.

I lie complacent, biting hard on the cotton in my mouth and trying to yell at the top of my lungs—not that it's very loud with the gag. My face is soaked with tears, my beautiful satin pillows damp beneath my head.

"I see you've chosen the easy way. Shame."

Daring to open my eyes, I am faced with something I never thought I'd hate to see. He's jacking off, and it has to be the ugliest dick I've ever seen in my life. Fuck knows why I'm fixating on his dumpling of a cock, but at the moment I can't do much else.

"You like that, don't you." It's not a question. Quickly averting my gaze from the horror show standing next to the bed, I look up into the man's eyes as they burn holes into my face. That's when I see the switchblade. I watch in slow motion as he brings it to my cheek and wipes my own blood onto my skin.

If looks could kill, he'd have died a thousand painful deaths from my glare alone.

"There's that fire. I thought you'd lost it. Got quite boring for a while there. Come on, little whore, spit at me, curse at me... Fight. Me." That sinister grin returns to his face, his mud-brown eyes crinkling at the corners.

The fight in me hasn't left, but I refuse to give him the satisfaction, so I continue to think of ways he could die. It's dark as fuck, but that's where I am right now. I'm scared, I'm in a shit ton of pain, but now I'm angry, too.

Fucking seething.

His breathing gets heavier as his hand moves faster on his stubby dick. He leans his head down to my thigh where the thousand papercuts are throbbing, and licks at the blood trickling from the wound. Feeling pressure applied to the cut—or however the fuck he's mutilated me down there—sends a scream tearing through me. There's no holding it back. It feels like he's ripping my skin off as his moans of pleasure get louder.

Tears flood my eyes, making it almost impossible to see. I'm close to passing out from the pain as he tugs one final time, on my skin and his penis. His cum spurts in jets over my now naked body—he must've removed my clothes while I was passed out.

"There we are. All done." He puts something on the bedside table with his switchblade before zipping up his pants. "Wanna see how good you look, little whore?" Picking up whatever he just put down, he rubs it across his cheek. It leaves a trail of blood right before he shoves it in my face... and I vomit right there. I almost choke as I have to swallow it back down, the gag still restricting me. It's a square patch of my skin, about an inch wide on either side.

Holy shit, that's my fucking thigh. That is skin. From. My. Thigh. I think I'm going to be sick again. But then my brain focuses on his low laugh.

A terrifying sound that will haunt my sleep for weeks.

"Now, I'm going to untie one of your arm restraints before I leave. I'm not a complete sadist. The rest you can figure out for yourself."

This is the first time I've found myself face to face with this kind of psychopath, and I don't fucking like it.

# CHAPTER EIGHT

## RIVER

I've been staring at this wall for what feels like a lifetime.

The room is dark—the sun set hours ago—and the black-out curtains make sure I lose myself in the nothingness.

I don't know the time. I don't know the day. I don't know how the fuck I got myself into this situation.

When I got home from my work loft, I avoided any lingering conversations with Mr. Bobby, telling him I was tired and needed my bed. He smiled, but he knew. He had to. I was broken and incapable of pretending otherwise.

Once in my apartment, I drew the curtains, turned off my phone, and headed straight for the shower.

The physical pain of cleaning up my wound was nothing compared to my bruised psyche.

Psyche.

Kai.

I needed him that night. I needed my best friend to hold me, to avenge me. I needed the boy I've loved my entire life to shield me from myself.

But once again, he shattered my heart when my body and mind were already teetering on the edge of sanity.

I blink away the new tears as I think of the phone call I made after my shower.

It was a short call. I know because the number of seconds it took for him to destroy me keeps running around in my mind like a fucking silent film.

Seven seconds.

One second to say hello.

One second to repeat the word.

One second to say my name in disdain.

The rest was white noise.

Seven seconds to bring me to my knees.

Fuck.

It's been long enough. I gave myself time to break down, now it's time to get my shit together and go back to my life. I've wallowed, I've reflected, I've holed myself up to the point that the hunger pain is greater than the sting on my thigh.

My thigh. Christ, I can't believe that psycho peeled off a square inch of my skin. Who fucking does that?

Slowly, I sit up and swing my legs to the side of the bed, my head hanging low. It feels like I've got the motherload of all hangovers but in reality, I'm not a drinker when bad shit happens to me. Though, to be honest, sometimes I wish I were so maybe I could forget shit, even if for a little while. But I don't because I need to have a clear head to over-analyze every detail of what happened to me. I have to look at it all from every angle so that next time, I'm prepared. I'm *better* prepared.

With a heaving sigh, I lift myself up to my full height and stretch my arms up above my head reveling in the feel of my cracking spine. Getting an appointment with my chiropractor should probably be on my list of priorities.

But first, I need to shower.

On my way to the bathroom, I grab the phone that's been sitting, dead to the world like me, on my nightstand. Pressing the side button, it still doesn't come to life which can only mean the battery is dead, which makes sense. It's not like I've taken the time to charge it since I've been back.

With my charger in hand, I plug it into the wall of the bathroom and sit on the toilet as I listen to the endless pings echoing in the small space.

It's my work phone, so the messages are mostly from the private app I have set up for my clients. Their secret identities secure, they message me with a code and that code corresponds to a person in my files.

I pee, I wipe, I wash my hands and the fucking thing is still pinging away. I suppose I'll be playing catch up for a while.

Once my hands are dry, I put in all the security codes and numbers before I can actually see what the fuck is happening.

Tyler has called twenty-three times and left as many text messages. The last one is frantic, telling me he's about to call the police but he doesn't have my real name, which is a problem when filing a missing person's report.

He's angry and I find myself relieved that someone actually noticed my absence.

*Kai.*

I glance toward my room where my private phone lies silent. I didn't turn it off but I'm guessing the battery is dead after... I look at the date and realize I've been holed up for a week.

*Jesus.*

A week of self-care and healing is apparently what I needed.

My thoughts go back to that night and as if on cue, my eyes travel straight to the inside of my thigh where a patch of missing skin has been replaced by a lump of crust. I may have been out of it for the last week but I was lucid enough to clean and disinfect my wound. My body is my greatest commodity. My money maker. I can't work if I'm scarred beyond redemption.

Goddammit.

Tyler is going to notice, of course. And I'd be an idiot to think he'll wait another week to see me.

I call him first so he'll stop worrying.

I barely hear the first ring before he answers. His voice is tight, severe, like he's trying his best to reel himself in.

"Excuse me, gentlemen. I'll be right back."

Did he just leave a meeting to answer my call? This is going to be bad, I can feel it.

I hear the slam of a door and then his voice again. This time there's a gentle undertone.

"Rose. Are you alright?" I can almost hear all the things he doesn't say.

*I've been worried.*

*Where have you been?*

*Are you hurt?*

He can't actually ask all of those questions, it's not what we're about. I don't owe him my private life but I feel like I should ease his mind anyway.

"I'm fine, Tyler. I'm sorry I haven't answered my phone. The battery died." It's the truth.

"For a week?" There's the boardroom king.

"It's... complicated. But I promise, I'm fine now." My gaze is fixed on the mirror while I try to convince Tyler that I haven't been a broken pile of nothingness for the past seven days. Taking inventory of my appearance, I wince at the mess in front of me. My eyes are puffy from the crying, my skin is ashy, my hair a flat, lifeless mop on top of my head.

Even my lips are chapped.

I'm so far removed from looking like an escort that I ask myself if maybe I should look for another career. Another path.

"Rose." Tyler's commanding voice pulls me out of my musings and has my eyes focusing on anything but the reflection in the mirror.

"Yes, sorry. I was reading something." It's not really a lie, I was reading my features, making sure I'm okay. Checking on myself.

Because that's what responsible fucking adults do.

"So, we're agreed?" *Oh fuck.*

"Um, I kinda zoned out there for a second, Tyler. I'm sorry, what did you ask?" The billionaire CEO hates repeating himself but he does anyway, and I can hear the frustration in his voice tinged with a bit of concern. This is not me. I'm a fucking professional and I need to get my shit together.

"I need you here tomorrow night, and then next week for a charity golf event. Can you fit me in?" How could I deny him? Just those two nights are going to almost make up for the week off.

"Of course." I sigh, knowing he's going to have questions I cannot answer as soon as he sees my wound.

"Good. I'll have my car pick you up at six. No need to go all out for tomorrow night. It's just us, but I need to blow off some steam."

"Sounds good. I'll be ready."

We hang up with plans all ready to go.

The shower is long and hot. I stand under the powerful jet of water for long minutes, like I'm washing away my sorrow and my pain. Like the water is cleansing me of my sins and the wrongs done to me. Like I'll be walking away brand fucking new.

It's all a lie, an illusion, of course. But it doesn't matter. I need it. I need to feel reborn so I can walk out of this apartment not feeling like the goddamn victim I am.

No, not a victim.

I'm a fucking survivor.

The next day, I'm stopped at the steps of my building just before the car arrives.

"Miss River, let me look atchou." I knew this was coming.

"Hi, Mr. Bobby. Been awhile." Shit, he's got that look in his eyes and now I'm praying for the car to get here fast so I can have an excuse to get the fuck out of dodge.

"You alright? I'm not the kinda man who's up in people's business but you didn't look right the other day." Oh, this sweet man. I suppose that night my feelings were out front and center.

"Yes, just a little misunderstanding. You know, affairs of the heart and all." He doesn't look convinced but luck is on my side when the car quietly pulls up to the curb.

"River?" I turn expectantly at the concern lining the big man's voice. Looking at him with his scruffy beard that, with a little tender loving care, could give Santa Claus a run for his money, I notice his eyes don't hold his usual laugh lines. He's serious and worried, and I feel the need to reassure him.

"Mr. Bobby, I promise—" He cuts me off, his voice low and hard.

"Is he hurting you? I saw blood, River."

Oh my God.

The shock must be visible because his hard tone softens.

"Okay, okay. Just promise me you will tell me if you ever need help. I won't take no for an answer." Well, I guess that settles that.

I take two steps back toward him, where he always sits, day in and day out, and kiss him on the cheek. "I promise, Mr. Bobby."

He takes my hand and squeezes it—a pointed look my way—like he's reiterating his previous words.

I smile, this time with sincerity written all over it.

As I step down toward the car, Aaron is there opening the door for me. Tall and military-like with his crew cut and steel spine, he's always been a quiet force. Not much of a talker but his watchful eyes have always intrigued me.

"Thank you, Aaron." I smile, grateful for his treatment of me even though he's in the know. I've never once felt judged, but I suppose he knows his boss's needs are un-orthodox.

It's when I look inside the car that I gasp.

Sitting there, oozing sex and power, is none other than Tyler fucking Walker, watching me intently as one bare leg steps in. I shiver at the way his gaze travels up from my ankle to my calf and zeroes in between my thighs, making me instantly wet.

He looks like an urban king as he sits, legs spread, head low, eyes raised and filled with lust, with a rocks glass hanging from two nimble fingers.

"Tyler, I wasn't expecting you." My voice is breathy, surprise clear in the hitch of my last word.

"It was a last-minute decision," he leans forward, his free hand outstretched for me to take. As soon as I'm inside, Aaron closes the door, and Tyler gently pulls me to him until I'm straddling his suit-covered thighs, my skirt bunched at my waist. "Hmm, and it was the right one to make."

Taking a sip from his glass, he places it in the cup holder before dipping two of his fingers inside the dark hon-ey-colored liquid.

Holy shit, I know how much that whiskey costs but he couldn't give a damn.

Those same two fingers come up to my mouth and, like he's coating them in lipstick, he circles my top then bottom lip before taking me into a hot, deep kiss that makes my toes curl and my core clench with need.

"I've thought about this for days. You made me wait." His mouth is back on mine as his hand squeezes around the red-haired wig and pulls me in for a deeper, more intense kiss. He takes his time, licking up and down, sucking on my tongue, biting my bottom lip. He's hungry and it has nothing to do with food. "Nobody makes me wait. Yet, here I am, in this fucking car because when it comes to you, I apparently have no patience."

As he speaks, I can feel his cock growing harder and harder behind his zipper. The thought that I can make this larger-than-life man drop his billion-dollar meetings for a moment inside me is quite heady. A girl could get used to this kind of undivided attention.

Already he's making my wallowing week disappear, if only for an hour. Or a night. That said, I need to be careful. He's not my knight nor is he my savior.

He's my client. Nothing more, nothing less.

"I guess I better make it up to you, then?"

"Take my cock out." His voice has hardened, his words leaving no room for denial.

Not that I would deny him. He calls the shots. Always. It's in the contract.

Reaching down, I deftly unbutton and pull down the zipper, watching as his hard dick springs free.

Commando. Not surprising, really.

Looking back at him, I wait for further instructions after checking that the partition between us and Aaron is locked and tinted.

He finishes off his command by handing me a square foil packet that I know he wants me to pull over his cock.

I love doing this. There's a kind of thrill at being the one to sheathe a powerful man's dick. Putting it in a cage, of sorts. Stopping it from proliferating.

The foil tears easily between my teeth, our eyes never wavering, our bodies grinding with only my panties to separate us.

"Don't play, Rose. It's been too long."

Pinching the tip, I slide the rubber down and, as soon as it reaches his root, I pull my panties to the side and sink onto him.

We both moan at the hot feel of us. My pussy squeezes his cock as he takes my wrists and places them at the small of my back.

I hesitate, the memory of a week ago flashing in my mind's eye. I try to push it away but Tyler feels my reluctance. It only lasts a half second but he didn't become the most powerful man in Manhattan by ignoring his gut.

"What's wrong? Did I hurt you?" We went from scolding hot to arctic cold in the lapse of one movement.

"No, no. It was a small cramp." Fuck, I hope I'm a good liar.

He doesn't move for longer than I like but eventually—after searching my gaze for interminable minutes—he resumes his initial plan.

His mouth latches onto my tits, one nipple then the other, sucking them into his mouth, shirt and all. When he releases me, I've got two wet spots on either breast. I feel dirty but also sexy as fuck.

"Ride me. Make me come before we reach the penthouse." His voice is even, like he's ordering hors-d'oeuvres, but I catch the slight hitch as I lift just enough to have the tip still inside but the shaft exposed to the air. Then I sink down and grind my clit against the manicured hair that surrounds his root.

"That's it, Rose. Give it to me." He brings his thumb to my mouth, pushing it between my lips and rubbing it against my tongue while I suck on it like it's my last meal.

When he's satisfied, he brings it to my clit and turns languid circles around the hard nub in rhythm with my rising and falling movements.

I'm moaning now, feeling the familiar stirring in my lower belly, the impending orgasm that he requires of me.

Also in the contract.

He insisted that my pleasure not take the back seat—no pun intended.

I'm guessing we're not too far from his apartment because his patience flies out the window as he reaches up and rips my button-down shirt wide open, pulling down the cups of my bra and sucking on my nipples. Deep and forceful. It almost hurts, but the pleasure is greater.

"Yes, fuck. Yes, Tyler." It's rare that I let myself lose a little control, but I need this. I need to feel wanted and desired. I need to feel beautiful while the disgusting wound on my thigh heals.

Tyler takes the swell of my breast into his mouth and with a fervor that he rarely shows, he sucks hard enough I'm sure it'll leave a mark.

I'm too far gone to actually care. In fact, I scream at him to suck harder.

And he does as I ask on my other tit.

"Come, Rose. All over my fucking dick. Right now."

I don't know how he does it. I don't know why my body obeys so easily, but it does.

Seconds before the car pulls up to the curb of his Fifth Avenue penthouse, I cry out just as he brings my mouth down to his and swallows his name from my lips.

The moment is broken when his hand releases my wrists and lands on my thigh, his thumb pressing against the healing wound.

I jolt and gasp, the pain surprising me more than actually hurting.

"What's wrong?"

I'm like a deer in the headlights, frantically trying to find an excuse, a reason for my reaction to his touch.

It's stupid, really. It's not like he won't see it.

And he does. Probably feels the scab with his thumb.

"What the fuck is this, Rose?"

Well, this is going to be difficult to explain.

# CHAPTER NINE

## RIVER

It goes without saying, Tyler didn't take the information about what happened to me well. I know I didn't owe him answers, but it actually felt good to talk about it, to tell someone. The look that crossed his face—ever so briefly—when I told him the man's *name*, made me wish I hadn't said anything at all. But that was quickly forgotten after he gave me more orgasms than I can count.

The orgasms. Mmm. I really needed those.

Spending time with Tyler has given me some of my confidence back, and today I'm finally meeting with Polly.

*I'm a powerful, bad bitch.*

I repeat my new mantra as I check myself out in the floor-length mirror of my bedroom. My black Timberlands paired with my home-made jean shorts, a tank top, and my waist-length leather jacket are perfect for how I'm feeling. The scabby-looking wound on my thigh is visible, purely because I want Polly to see what her sloppiness allowed to happen.

My phone pings to let me know my Uber has arrived. Time to grab my bag and head on out. I don't want to have this conversation with Polly, she's done a lot for me in the past and I've always looked up to her, but she needs to know it wasn't okay and it won't be happening again.

Ever.

Arriving at the cute little wine bar doesn't take long. Polly waves me over to the fancy booth when she sees me walk in. Her long-time security guy, Frank, is sitting as discreetly as he can a few tables over. He's been with her for years, since before I started working with her. I'd be surprised if they've never fucked; it can't be *all* business with those two. I mean, I imagine having him around would be like having your own personal John Cena on standby. He's always freaked me the fuck out with the way he leers at the girls, but Polly seems to like him and, well, not my circus. Plastering on my best 'everything is fine' smile, I head on over to Polly.

"Darling, how are you? It's been so long." She rises from her seat to air-kiss both of my cheeks—her usual greeting.

"It has. How's business?" I'm not messing around with small talk today. I feel like there's a reason Polly's girls were 'sick' that night. From the shit that psychopathic moth-erfucker said, this wasn't the first time he's done this. I just hope Polly doesn't know about it, or every ounce of respect I have for the woman will fuck off down the toilet.

"No pleasantries today? Is everything okay, darling?" Genuine concern is clear on her face, putting me at ease.

"Not really, Polly. That Rex guy you sent to me last week, do you know much about him?" It's really difficult to not stutter his name, but I won't allow him to hold that power over me, and I'm happy I said it clearly.

"Not a lot. One of the regulars sent him our way. Said he was a friend." She looks worried now. Since I never usually question her about clients, I think realization is setting in. "Rose? Darling, tell me what happened." Her spine stiffens, and her shoulders roll back as if she's readying herself for a fight. She places her weathered hand on mine, her green eyes boring steadfast as she awaits a response.

It takes me a moment to gather myself, but after speak-ing with Tyler the other night, this is a lot easier than I imagined it would be. She knows what's coming, I can tell from the tightness around her mouth.

After a few wines, and a long explanation—I don't spare her any details—she's up from her seat and holding me tight. This reaction confirms she knew nothing. I hate that I doubted her for even a second.

"We need some stronger drinks than wine, darling. I think cocktails are in order."

Four in the fucking morning. That's when Aaron pulled up to my apartment to take Tyler and me to the charity golf tournament. Tyler's lucky he's pretty. That, and he pays well.

I opted for white, wide-leg pants today, paired with a white tank top and white sheer blouse. My red wig has been styled into a sleek side-bun with a few loose tendrils around my lightly made-up face. Sophistication is key at Tyler's events. It's all about the aesthetics.

These golf cart things are a lot more fun than they look in the movies, though the actual golf part of today is about as much fun as a kick in the shins.

"Ooh, can I drive the cart?" I sidle up to Tyler on our way to the final hole of the day, my hand on his thigh as I look up to him sweetly.

"Behave." He side-eyes me as my hand slowly climbs higher.

"Come on, I just wanna drive the cart. Please?"

"I'll drive into your pussy if you don't stop asking." The growl he emits as he speaks is intense, and it sends a delicious tingle straight between my legs.

"You're no fun." I over-exaggerate my pout as I continue to slide my palm up and down his firm thigh.

Tyler slows the cart to a stop, turns to face me just as his fingers pinch my chin and his mouth comes to my ear. "I dare you to say I'm no fun later when my dick is pummeling your pussy so hard you'll beg me to make you come." Jesus. I really like this dominant side of him. "We've got one last hole on the course and then, after the gala, I'll play with every single one of your holes." I'm so fucking wet right now, I'm afraid the white pants won't hide any of it. "Now, be a good girl and I'll make you come before we leave here."

These conversations with Tyler are one of my favorite parts of the job. It's so easy to forget he's paying me to be here with the effortless way our bodies react to each other. In another life, I could absolutely see myself with this man.

We arrive at the final hole and two of Tyler's colleagues and their wives in their own cart pull up behind us. I'm grateful we weren't paired with Brett and Cora for today, it surely would've put a damper on the whole thing. I know we have to mingle with them at the gala this evening, but to have the day without them has been blissful.

The giggling wives exit their cart, fawning over their husbands who are deciding which driver to use for this hole. Tyler helps me stand before getting what he needs, pulling me over to him and handing a club to me.

"Er, Tyler?" I'm confused right now. I know I've just stood and watched him dominate the last seventeen holes but why the fuck is he passing me the club?

"Thought you might like to have a shot." A mischievous glint passes through his eyes as he places the ball on the tee.

Fuck it, why not?

"Okay, but I don't have a clue what I'm doing. Can you help?" Flirting with Tyler comes so naturally, his colleagues would never guess this is all part of a service.

A slow grin creeps onto his god-like face, his strong jawline pronounced as he looks at me with intensity before he spins me and wraps his arms around me from behind. He leisurely slides his fingers down from my shoulders to my wrists, where I'm holding the club with both hands. His cock is resting against my lower back as he helps me adjust my grip on the handle, his lips so close to my ear I have to suppress a shudder.

"Move your feet shoulder width apart."

I do as he instructs, while also pushing out my ass more than necessary into his crotch. The low growl that follows gives me a satisfied smile.

"Yeah, just like that. Now keep your eye on the ball, and I'll help you." He clears his throat before moving my arms up and to the side, ready to swing down and hit the ball.

It goes quite far, so far that it lands on the green, and I turn to wrap my arms around Tyler's neck, planting an excited kiss on his luscious lips.

"That was quite the shot there, young lady. Tyler's clearly a great coach." Graham—the tallest of the two men we've been paired with today—lets out an almighty laugh as he grabs his own wife by the waist and whispers in her ear. Whatever it is, she likes it as she starts giggling like a schoolgirl while he burrows his face into her neck.

"That he is, Graham. That he is." I allow my hand to slide down Tyler's back, resting it just above his ass with my head against his chest as we watch Thomas take his shot to the green.

"You're gonna pay for that little ass trick as soon as I get you alone." It's not a promise he's whispering into my ear, it's a threat. I can't help but be excited about how Tyler plans on 'punishing' me.

"Why wait until we're alone?" I sass back at him, lowering my hand discreetly so it's now fully on his ass.

"Getting cocky now, are we?" His low voice paired with a smug grin are the perfect panty-melting combination. That, and the fact that he's richer than God are reasons he likes to pay for my company. With me, he knows what he's getting. He knows I'm not trying to marry him for his money or contacts. I'm just doing my job, and we have fun while we're at it. This is why we work.

I raise a brow at him, a half-smile playing on my lips as my hand finds its way to his lower back, skirting the top of his ass with my fingertips. True to form, he responds with a low growl, like the refined savage that he is. Whoever ends up with this man for life will be a very lucky lady indeed.

Thomas and Graham are finished with their initial shots, so we all climb back into the carts and head over to the green so they can finish the game. Sitting in the passenger side, Tyler leaves the driver's side for me to slide into.

On the short ride to the green, Tyler slips his hand down the front of my pants to slowly rub at my clit before dipping a finger inside me. It only lasts a few moments before we arrive, and as soon as we do, he removes his finger and puts it to my lips. He nudges them open as he slowly slides his finger inside my mouth, and I willingly suck myself off him, flicking my tongue over the tip of his finger.

We keep eye contact for a brief second before he's up and choosing his putter for this last shot. If we make it back to the room after this without fucking, I'll be surprised.

"So, how long have you known Tyler?" It's the first time one of these women has spoken to me all day. They've kept to themselves and their own cart mostly, giggling and chatting with each other, happily ignoring my existence. I get it, I'm not one of the elite. I'm not in their circle. All they know of me is what they've seen at corporate events and gatherings—and I'm okay with that.

I plaster on a fake smile before answering, remembering the back story we agreed to as part of the contract. "A while." I lower my gaze slightly, as if I'm shy when talking about my relationship with Tyler. "We've known each other for a few years, and recently we decided to make a go of it."

The brunette sneers at me, nudging the one with cropped blonde hair lightly before plastering on her own fake smile. It'd be nice to meet some genuine women at these events, but I guess that's why Tyler hires me, so he doesn't have to deal with these unbearable snobs.

"So, are you the reason he broke it off with Cora?" The brunette stares at me, her synthetic lips pursed in accusation.

I'm about to snark back at the bitch before the blonde gently rests a hand on my arm and leans in.

"Don't worry about her, she's all up in Cora's ass."

I give her a thankful smile and turn to her friend.

"Not that it's any of your business, but no. Tyler and I got together after his wife cheated on him with his best friend. You know, the guy she's with right now."

"Well that's not the story Cora told us, is it?" She looks to her friend for backup. But she gets none.

"Jessica, let it go." The blonde turns to give me a subtle wink as the men come back over to join us.

Tyler and I walk back over to our cart. Behind me, I can hear *Jessica* making snide remarks, but fuck it. Not my circus.

A few minutes later, Tyler has said his goodbyes to Thomas, Graham, and their wives. We're now on our way to park the cart before heading up to our room to change for the gala this evening.

Only, we're not going in the right direction, we're heading toward some kind of utility shed that's between a big hill and a small lake.

"Tyler, where are we going?" I'm not worried, just curious.

"You didn't think I was going to give you your punishment in the comfort of our room, did you?" The lustful grin that spreads over his face reminds me of how damp I already am. "Switch places with me."

"While we're moving?"

He doesn't answer, just raises a brow and gives me a "Go ahead, defy me" look.

It's not going particularly fast, but the small thrill of switching places while the cart is moving—rubbing against his cock as I do—has me laughing and forgetting that bad shit ever happens.

Tyler still controls the cart—even though I'm in the driver's seat—as he slips his hand inside my pants and starts those slow circles on my clit again.

Had he left me to drive on my own, we would've crashed. The delicious feeling that is building inside me doesn't allow me control of my own body, let alone a moving vehicle.

He's on me as soon as we stop.

"Take off your pants and rest your hands on the front of the cart."

Flushed, my eyes fix on his as I slowly pull down my pants, leaving my bottom half bare to him as I follow his instructions and place my hands on the cart.

Of course I've gone commando; white clothes show everything and visible panties are unacceptable in these circles.

Poking out my ass and arching my back, I look over my shoulder to see Tyler stalking toward me with a hungry look in his eyes. We're reasonably hidden away behind the shed, so I'm not worried about getting caught.

"Turn around, eyes front."

"Yes, sir." *Oh I like where this is going.*

"Good girl." Grabbing my legs, he nudges them apart before his tongue licks a slow trail from my ankle, all the way up to my center. He takes special care to avoid my scar with his tongue, but he does place a gentle kiss there as he passes it.

Tyler takes his time, licking me from clit to ass, swirling his tongue in the most delicious of ways. Every flick sends a jolt up my spine, almost causing my legs to buckle. One, then two fingers are added to the party, as he slowly inserts them inside me. He bends them just right, hitting that sweet spot, and it's oh so fucking amazing.

My building orgasm feels like a tsunami as it overwhelms me, and he puts his thumb in my ass, sending me completely over the edge.

"Oh my fucking God, Tyler. Yes." My screams can probably be heard across the golf course, but I really don't give a shit. And I know Tyler doesn't either.

He laps up everything I give him before standing and unbuckling his belt. Turning to stare at him again over my shoulder, I smile, fascinated by the glint of my cum on his lips and chin.

"Eyes forward, Rose."

I hear the rustling of the condom wrapper moments before he thrusts inside me, his hands tight on my hips. He's relentless as he takes his fill, the only sounds are our bodies slapping together mixed with moans of pleasure.

Reaching around to my front, he palms my breast, taking the nipple between his fingers as he pinches and twists. His teeth graze my shoulder and throat as he continues to pound into me, and I can already feel another orgasm building.

This is hard and fast... and I fucking love it.

Tyler's movements become erratic as he nears his own orgasm, hitting that sweet spot inside me on every single push. The tingling sensation grows from the very tips of my toes to each hair on my head, and on his final, deep thrust, his growl of satisfaction sends fireworks straight to my clit. My screams of pleasure are drowned out as he places a hand over my mouth and I suck on his fingers.

"What's going on out here?" An aged voice calls over from the window of the utility shed the cart is parked against.

"Shit." Tyler pulls out, removing the condom and handing me my pants as we giggle like children caught raiding the cookie jar.

We can't see who it is, but I know Tyler doesn't want to wait to find out. We're back on the cart and ready to move in no time as I try to put my pants back on.

"Hurry up, Rose. No one gets to see you like this. Only me."

He takes my hand and pulls me and my trembling legs onto his lap before driving away.

There's just something about what he said that's bothering me. I'm a little worried about his reaction. He knows I'm an escort, so obviously other people are going to see me naked and in the midst of an orgasm. If he had said this as part of our contract in front of his colleagues, I would've understood, but there was no one around—other than the guy who disturbed us.

Maybe it's time to stop seeing Tyler. It won't work if he gets too attached.

There's just something about him though, and the way he treats me makes me feel invincible.

Do I really want that to stop?

# CHAPTER TEN

## RIVER

When I was little, my life was every child's dream. We lived on a plot of land not too far from Allison Park that my dad inherited from my grandfather. There was nothing there except tall trees and a bumpy clearing, the water too far to be heard sloshing against the coast.

Our parents weren't always like this, they came from middle class homes, even went to New York University which is where they met. But sometime during the nineties, they started following the music festivals—The Grateful Dead, Phish, The Allman Brothers and the like—and created some crazy as shit bonds with those they met there. My mother was smart but also crafty, making clothes and jewelry to sell at the shows, providing them with enough gas and food money to make it to the next one.

It was in ninety-seven, when I was about a year old, that they inherited my grandfather's land after he died. As the only living kin, my dad got everything. Instead of creating a home life like the rest of America, my parents lived to the beat of their own beliefs.

They brought back their friends, and on that land they placed nine mobile homes in a big circle, where we all ate and lived together like one big happy fucking family.

The only reason I didn't lose my fucking mind was because Kai was there. We were all homeschooled by my mom who'd double majored in Literature and Education. She'd often say that, had she lived the life her capitalist parents had wished for her, she would have been a teacher.

I never met any of my grandparents. Anytime I asked my mom about them, she'd tell me they weren't understanding people and didn't deserve to bathe in my light. But I'd heard her tell my dad they were assholes who ruled their home with a painful fist.

Despite all of my wary feelings toward the way my parents had chosen to live their lives, the one time of year that I always loved was the Harvest Moon festival. It was an all-day affair where we planned out our time, decorated, cooked, laughed and enjoyed just... being. Living. Thanking the universe for everything good in our lives.

Even as a cranky teen I could see the beauty of that night.

Between the six families, there were nine kids of all ages. Everest was my responsibility when we played, but Kai made it a point to help me. Freya, who was a few months younger than me, was my best friend, but Kai was my forever friend.

Or so I thought.

The Uber drops me off at my brother's place, which is just a few miles away from where we grew up. The old Hippie Farm—as the neighbors had dubbed our commune—is now holding four cookie-cutter homes where our childhood tree houses only exist in our memories.

The one thing we all agreed on when we went our separate ways was the Harvest Moon Festival.

Now that Everest and Petal have a home with a decent amount of land by Staten Island standards—*if only he knew how many blowjobs their house cost*—we promised to keep this one tradition alive.

So here I am, at the butt crack of dawn—seven in the morning on a Friday—to help my sister-in-law set up the decorations and make the apple pies. All organic, of course.

"River!" Petal's voice is soft and embracing, like her name. All velvety and warm. Exactly like her hugs, which she's lavishing upon me right now.

"Hey, Pet." I squeeze her to me and thank the gods she came into Everest's life, even though they are so young. She helps him focus. Ev's such a free spirit, but Petal is the love of his life, and he takes his responsibility of making sure she's happy seriously. He still refuses to have a corporate job or even work for the capitalist devils, whoever *they* may be. It's frustrating, sometimes, when I think back to everything I've sacrificed for him to be happy. But then, I remember the promise I made when our parents lay dead in the crashed car—blood running over the dashboard, eyes open and looking at each other with no hope of survival.

I promised him he'd be happy again. Happy and healthy. And maybe, just maybe, I'd feel less guilty.

Nine years and endless clients later, I can say I've kept my promise. The problem is, the sale of his produce isn't going to pay the house off.

I am.

He pays for the electric and all the utilities, but the house... it's on me. And that's okay. It's my burden to carry.

"So, I've sorted the apples. All the ingredients are here for the pies and there's a table ready with the crafts. I'm so excited! This will be our first Harvest Moon in our new home. Can you believe it? Okay, so what would you rather do, cook or craft?" Her smile is infectious so I do what we're supposed to do this time of year.

I give her a genuine grin and choose the crafts table. "Cooking is too stressful, I'll cut and paste instead."

"Thank the goddess, I'm much better at cooking." Petal was raised as the perfect little homemaker. She's good at everything she puts her mind to.

"Where's Ev?" I ask, but I'm guessing he's out getting wood for the fire pit. I look over the materials on the table, a familiar warmth burning in my chest at the sight of the old book pages lying in one pile and a stack of leaves in another.

Our tradition is to find a copy of a book that best describes our year—whether positive or negative—and rip out the pages. On them, we glue a leaf then attach all the pages together with a hemp cord, making our own garlands. Then we drape them on the trees around the fire pit. The idea is to tell the universe that either our last year was difficult and we are working on making some positive changes, or our year was amazing and we are taking stock on how to keep our good fortune.

I chose *The Seven Husbands of Evelyn Hugo*. As difficult as her life is in the story, there's just something good about her existence that I hang on to. My life isn't shit. It's not ideal, I know, but it's my own.

"He's at the farmer's market. He wanted to get the rest of the apples sold before tonight." Petal's voice always has a dreamy sound to it when she talks about my brother. It's cute. And naive in all the best of ways.

"Right, makes sense."

We get down to business, her breaking a sweat with each crust she makes from fucking scratch, and me cutting, gluing, and linking pages together with the hemp. It's mindless work, almost all muscle memory from our childhood, but it allows me to drift away into my thoughts while Trey Anastasio—the lead singer of Phish—belts out lyrics on the mostly-upbeat *AC/DC Bag*.

Jesus, the memories his voice provokes almost bring tears to my eyes. I work fucking hard at pushing away the images of my parents to the deep, dark recesses of my mind. I can't. I cannot function if I'm constantly allowing their smiling faces and midnight dances around the fire to cloud my consciousness.

The truth is, for all her free love mentality, my mother was a hardcore believer in fidelity; to her husband, but also to her self.

*"Be true to who you are, River. Your 'self' is the only thing that belongs to only you."*

Oh how disappointed she would be if she knew who my "self" turned out to be.

I wipe a stray tear from my cheek using my sleeve before it has time to fall onto the paper and sniff away my memories. Today is about new beginnings, about taking stock and planning for the new year.

Today is about celebrating life and everything it has offered during the plentiful months before the proverbial hibernation season begins.

"Having fun, Rose?" I jump so high, my thigh slams into the table and I curse at the sudden pain.

"What the fuck, Kai?" I place a palm on my battering heart and give him a look that could cut off his balls. He's used to it though and it doesn't even faze him. "And don't call me that." This time I whisper-yell, glancing over to a blissfully unaware Petal, who's placing her apple slices around and around with a satisfied grin on her pretty face.

"Why not? Are you ashamed of your boyfriend?" He says that last word like it personally offends him.

"Shut up, it's not like that." I rub at my leg, trying to ease the inevitable bruise that will be there tonight.

"Page Six begs to differ." He leans in and whispers in my ear, the hurt so clear it jabs a dagger straight to my heart. "Wedding bells are in the air." Then he's gone and I struggle to get breath into my lungs.

"Hey, Sis! Shit, that looks freaking fantastic." I look over at Everest as he languidly makes his way to me, a quick kiss on my cheek that tells me he's been generous with the reefer already.

"You smell like weed," I mutter, playfully pushing him away. I'll dab in the occasional joint but I stopped smoking daily the day after my parents died. Unfortunately, it was around that time that Everest really started. I mean, my parents smoked on the regular, even grew their own organic plants, so how hypocritical would it have been of me to try and stop him? I wish they'd seen the day the first legal cannabis store had opened their doors.

They died four days before the official legalization of marijuana in Denver. Four fucking days.

"That I do, big sister, that I do." When his eyes land on his wife, his grin grows even wider and his steps get a little quicker as he makes his way to her and wraps his big arms around her tiny frame. I watch, like a fucking voyeur, as they whisper sweet things to each other, their bubble so firmly in place it's almost disgusting.

With a sigh, I turn back to my task and from the corner of my eye, I see Kai tilting a bottle of beer to his lips.

"It's only ten in the morning." I don't actually care, but fuck I love his voice.

"Celebrating our stand being sold out. Those apples were a huge success." His eyes bore into me, staring at me like he's trying to figure me out.

"What? Why are you looking at me like that?" My fists punch into my jean-clad hips and I cock my head like a petulant child.

"No reason, really." He takes another sip, his eyes still on me. "Just trying to figure out when you sold out to the big man." Oh, this again.

"I didn't sell out, Kai. Fuck, let it go, okay? I'm allowed to date whoever the fuck I want." The lie feels like acid on my tongue.

"Hey, Ev. Did you know,"—that fucker is going to ruin Harvest Moon—"River, here, is going to golf charities and big uppity galas with none other than Tyler fucking Walker." He's talking to my brother, but he's looking straight at me with a challenge glinting in his eyes, daring me to deny it. Pushing me to fight him on this. He *wants* to be wrong.

"No, that's not possible." Petal's confused voice doesn't break the silent fight Kai and I are having. "She's in lo—"

My sister-in-law's comment is cut short by a voice I haven't heard in months. Thank fuck for that because if she had said what I think she would have said, I was walking out of here.

"Hey everyone! Sorry I'm late, but I had to drop by work to get my boss lady to sign a few things. Am I interrupting something?" I look over to the new addition to our party, and my blood runs cold.

Well, maybe I will be leaving after all.

"No, not at all. We were just discussing River's new beau." I don't miss the shutters in his gaze—the usually-open windows to his soul suddenly closed off—as he comes closer to me, places his empty beer bottle in the recycling bin next to me, then walks off with Freya Murphy.

Kai's ex-girlfriend.

My ex-best friend.

Our old commune family member.

Squaring my shoulders and raising my chin, I vow not to let her presence ruin my Harvest Moon.

# CHAPTER ELEVEN
## RIVER

By this time in our lives, setting up for the festivities is basically second nature. I decide to be an adult about this love triangle situation and suck it up. After all, it would be out of character for me to ignore Freya since no one—not a single other soul except myself—knows what I saw, when I saw it, and the fact that Freya—my best friend at the time—was well aware of my intentions of declaring my feelings to Kai.

I've been pretending it's all just fine, fine, fine since that awful night, but inside I was devastated. The problem is, since that night, they've been dating on and off for years. They'll fall into bed together, date for a couple of months because Freya doesn't want to feel like a slut—her words not mine—and then, inevitably, they'll break up because Kai isn't giving her the attention she deserves. Again, her words.

I'm over it. In fact, I'm pretty sure they'll fuck tonight, in the morning they'll be all over each other like newlyweds, and by the Winter Solstice it'll be off again. Lather, rinse, repeat.

As I bring out the last of the giant pillows and warm blankets, I have a fleeting thought about my Candy Aisle Guy. Nathaniel's face flashes in my mind just as I drop the load I'm carrying onto the grass. His smile makes my heart beat increase just the tiniest bit as I arrange the covers and fluff the pillows. The cerulean of the fabric matches the exact color of his eyes, making the corners of my mouth rise just enough for me to feel a little bit of warmth in my chest. All around me, the sounds of paper and crystals swaying in the light breeze remind me of the feel of soft breath on my skin.

"Shit, man. Did we do it on purpose?" Frowning, I turn to my brother and consider maybe he's too high to continue setting anything up.

"What do you mean?" I look around, trying to see things from his perspective.

"Holy shit." Kai's low murmur is closer to me than I expect, earning him a small gasp from me.

"It's exactly the same." Now, it's Freya's wonderment that's joined the mix and I'm just confused.

It's only when I step back and look at the scene in front of us that I understand. My heart swells behind my ribcage, the familiar ache of missing my parents all-consuming as I realize we've set up the entire scene like our parents before us. It's a miniature version, sure, but it's exactly the same pattern.

The fire pit in the middle and six bundles of blankets and giant pillows—color coded for each of the families back then—are meticulously arranged around the now-growing fire. I'm standing at what would have been my family's bundle—oranges and browns with a touch of cream.

We're all quiet for a moment until Petal's voice breaks the reminiscent trance we're drowning in from the memories of our past lives.

"Okay, here's the last of it!" Everest is the first to move, helping his wife to carry the pies and a bowl of water that we blessed earlier, which now needs to sit in the moonlight.

I feel him before I hear the words at my ear. "Remember, River, we always share a blanket." His pinky caresses the heart-shaped beauty mark at my neck, and he fucking knows it makes me pliable. Makes me soft. But even his touch can only go so far.

"Well, I'm sure Freya would have something to say about that." I turn to him and smile like the world is a-okay. His sigh is barely discernible and the glance over my shoulder discreet, but I know him. The last thing Kai wants is to hurt anyone, but right now he's torn between what's familiar and what's easy.

I'm the latter, apparently.

"Excuse me, I need to grab the paper and pens for the *Wish on the Ash*." I linger just a second longer than I should, reading his dilated pupils tinged with wariness and lust. The downward curve of his lips and the crease between his brows. Is he regretting inviting Freya? Or is he coming to grips with the fact that we are no more? Never actually were... anything? In my heart, I've always blamed Freya for coming between us, but for fuck's sake, we're adults and he and I have had years to make a decision.

But then my job has always been my barrier, hasn't it? How could I possibly have any type of relationship with Kai while fucking other men for cash? I can't. I won't. Even if he gave me permission—which he abso-fuck-ing-lutely would never—I still wouldn't want my two worlds to co-exist. The mere fact that he knows anything about Tyler is making my anxiety skyrocket.

It takes a while, but we're all finally settled in our blankets. Everest and Petal are snuggling, sharing a piece of apple pie and whispering sweet nothings to each other—or maybe filthy nothings, who the fuck knows? Lianna and Becca, Petal's sister and her wife, are right across the fire from me, and to my right is Kai. He's alone, which shouldn't make me so fucking happy, but it does, and on his other is side is Freya looking more sad than joyful. I wouldn't be surprised if we wore the same facial expressions. After all, we're both pining for the same man.

Correction. *She's* pining, I'm coming to grips with the never-could-be of my life.

"Okay, everyone. It's time." Petal's mother, Marie, begins. As the oldest, her and Peter will preside over the rituals. I'm glad because I'm in no emotional shape to lead this thing. The idea of doing it once they pass is bad enough. I have time though, thank fuck. "Mother Nature has blessed us with a cloudless sky and our sister, the moon, is gorgeous as ever, bathing us in her light."

I scoot up under my blankets and cross my legs, tilting my head back and facing the moon. There's something about this position that soothes me. It calms me. A bit like when Tyler takes the reins and fucks the worries right out of me.

Ugh. Okay, I need to concentrate.

Moon. Light. Ritual. Bathing. All the fucking moon-bathing.

"Let us close our eyes and face the moon, accept her cleansing of our bodies, our minds, and our souls. This is a time for reflection. Let us take a minute of solitude to think back on the last twelve months and give our thanks to the bountiful mother that is our Nature."

My eyes closed, I picture the last year like a series of PowerPoint slides that cross my mind's eye. The men, the money, the dubious clients and the impossible situations. I allow myself to briefly ponder the most frightening part of my year, the violation and the pain, the utter helplessness on that fateful night with a client I never should have taken.

I think back on all the sex I've had—some satisfying, some coma-inducing—and all the opportunities my orgasms have provided my brother.

They say money doesn't buy you happiness, but enough of it can bring a worry-free smile to our faces.

I think about Kai; about the number of times I've let him kiss me, touch me; the times he's pulled me into tight, secluded spaces and fucked me until my legs couldn't hold me up. I think about the lies, the omissions, the ideas I let them create about what I really do in Manhattan. Why I live there and not here.

I can't tell them the truth about the rich, available clients ready to fuck me for the equivalent of a month's rent. I doubt they'd appreciate my brand of honesty.

Then I let it all go. I let the breeze take away the negative emotions and breathe in the clean positivity that I'll need for the coming new year.

My body freezes as the heat under my blanket turns to chill before transforming into an inferno. The rustling of the covers and pillows make me lose my train of thought, but the feel of a warm, hard body sidling up to me is what finally does me in.

"What are you doing?" I whisper so softly I hope only he can hear me.

"Shh," Kai's response is frustrating to say the least, but he's right. This is not the time to speak.

"Okay, that was great everyone. Did you feel the moonbeams cleanse you?" We all respond in various ways—some sigh out a *yes,* others grunt. It's me, I'm "others."

"Right, so let's present our wishes to the ashes. River has been so kind as to distribute recycled paper to everyone, they should be secured under a rock next to your pillows."

We all take out our papers and concentrate on the wishes we want to send out to the universe.

"What's your wish, River?" *Is it possible to want to punch and fuck a man at the same time?* Every year, since I can remember, Kai has asked me this question during our ritual. And every year I give him the same answer.

"To be able to eat meat." The double entendre only came to us in our later teens, but the first time I answered him I was being literal. I really, really wanted to know the taste of meat. Although I've long since given up veganism, my answer is still the same.

For the sake of memories.

"I've got your meat right here." We both chuckle at his ready answer, the same one he's given me since age sixteen.

I give him a side-eye, incapable of not smiling because, fuck me, when he grins with both dimples on proud display, I could seriously jump on his *meat* and not regret a damn thing.

"We are at your home, Everest and Petal. You do the honors." Everest smiles and places both of his hands on Petal's cheeks then kisses her with so much love I can feel its potency from where I sit. He rises and takes Petal's hand as they walk over to the fire. Standing behind her, they place the folded papers in their closed fists and kiss each other passionately as they drop the papers into the dancing flames. Wishes to ashes. The moon and the fire now hold their words for infinity.

I scribble one word on my paper. Just one. It's all I really need for this year. For this life, really.

"River, sweetheart, it's your turn." Petal's sweet mother nods to me and then to the fire pit.

I'm rising to my feet when Kai's hand on my forearm stops me. Looking over at him, I see the sincerity in his clear eyes. Clearer than they've been all night.

"Wish for me, River."

The word on my paper burns a hole in my palm. I lean in and kiss his cheek, my lips lingering long enough for me to inhale the earthy scent of him.

Rising, I smile down at his expectant face before forcing myself to walk to the fire. My hand extends, my heart constricts. I look over my shoulder at Kai right before my fingers open and the paper is engulfed by the flames. It's gone in a second, the power of the fire too great for my word.

*Clarity.* It's all I really want.

By the time the circle is complete, we spend the rest of the night talking and laughing and sharing our greatest memories. Petal and her family didn't know our parents so we regale them with stories of communal living and unorganized road trips while passing around an endless amount of weed. I rarely smoke anymore. In fact, I haven't since last Winter Solstice.

It's almost two in the morning when my bladder decides it cannot wait another second before exploding. I'm feeling good, worry-free. The permanent weight on my shoulders barely feels like a feather thanks to the hazy high that's clouding my mind.

We're past the laughing stage by now and have moved on to the silent contemplation stage, our inner thoughts like a complete conversation with ourselves. I'm solving world hunger by the time I make it to the bathroom, and by the time I've peed the equivalent of the Mississippi River, I think I've figured out how to eliminate capitalism with an equalitarian form of government. By the time I've washed my hands—even being high won't deter me from good hygiene—I'm convinced that the Harvest Moon has given me my wish.

I have clarity.

I know what I'm going to do. I have all the fucking solutions at the tip of my tongue.

Reaching out for the doorknob, my phone in hand, I laugh at Tyler's new message.

**Tyler:** I'm at the bar trying to close a deal but I keep thinking of you. Now I'm hard as nails

**Me:** It's the Harvest Moon

I don't have time to reach the door before it flies open and there stands Kai. He's glorious and determined. Lust is clear in his eyes but there's something else there, too. His jaw is clenched, his fists opening and closing in a steady rhythm like he's practicing his next words.

"Do you need to pee?" Stupid question, we're in the bathroom. I look around and frown. Everest should make it bigger, maybe put in a shower stall next to the tub. I prefer showers, they're cleaner. But baths are—

Fuck, I'm high.

"No, I don't need to pee." The space is so small that it only takes Kai two steps to have my back against the wall. "River." My name is a whisper from his lips that licks at my skin, my nerves, my soul.

With my eyes closed, I wish for another time or place or destiny. But then I remember his words.

*Wish for me, River.*

What if my word is just a synonym for Kai? What if he's my clarity? It would make sense.

"Kai." I say so much in that one word.

"Did you wish for me?" Opening my eyes, I'm met with liquid honey. The gold swirling with an intensity that makes my pussy clench, my body tremble with the need for him.

"I—"

My phone pings with an incoming message, shaking on the counter. We both look over to the lit-up screen and my clarity disappears in a puff of regret.

Tyler's name is flashing with an incoming call. Refusing him now is not a good idea. The man does not like to be ignored and it's in my contract that unless it's life threatening, I'm to answer his call... always.

"Don't. Ignore him, River. Don't answer." I was wrong. The moon didn't give me shit, but the fire may very well be consuming for a lifetime.

"I can't..." My eyes fix on Kai, begging him to understand even though he has no information, no real insight, as to why it's crucial that I answer. I pick up the call and as Tyler's voice fills my ears, I see the light burn out in Kai's gaze.

I thought we were done at the park so many nights ago. I was wrong.

Back then, hope was still in the air.

Tonight, that hope is crushed.

*Clarity.*

# CHAPTER TWELVE
## RIVER

My work phone pings, disturbing my peace and quiet as I chill in front of the TV with a glass of wine. There's nothing on, but it's mind-numbing enough to keep me from spiraling about what happened with Kai on Harvest Moon. I mean, it was a great night, but after that moment in the bathroom I felt something between us changed and I don't like it. Maybe it was unfair of me to expect him to wait forever.

Another ping from my phone reminds me I've got a new message. It's a request from a potential new client. Something else to keep myself busy and I can't complain.

After spending far too long researching and looking into his details, I send 'Elijah' a message. He now has the code allowing him to read through and sign the contract I've made up for him. Once that's complete, we can arrange our first 'date.'

I've managed to finish off two bottles of wine, and it's now past midnight. Kai's face crumbling is at the forefront of my mind as I now lie in my huge, soft bed. Alone. Forever alone. I wish I had the guts to just tell him, but I'm sure his face would just crumble for different reasons. Either way, I don't win.

I should be happy. I've got a full roster of clients, my brother and Petal are happy and thriving, and I'm living a very comfortable life. As much as I'm grateful for all that, I can't help but wonder where I'd be if I hadn't taken on the parent role with Ev. Or where we'd be if we didn't have to sell our parents' land to pay off their debts, leaving us struggling until I found Polly.

Would Kai and I have ever worked? Would the Freya thing still bother me, or is it just an excuse?

We've had disagreements before the other night, but none like that. There were no raised voices, no insults thrown, but Kai's whole aura changed. Almost like he was disappointed. Yeah, that's it, disappointment. He's disappointed to lose his regular fuck buddy is what it is. Never having an actual boyfriend always meant I was available to Kai whenever he wanted. And I always gave in to the nostalgia of being with him. Is that what it is? Nostalgia?

I don't fucking know.

What I do know, is that the world is currently spinning and I'm now regretting my second bottle of wine. And maybe the twelve-inch pizza too.

Sitting up slowly, because I'm desperate for a drink of water right now, I check my phone to see if Kai's replied to my message.

Nothing.

Of course not. Why would he let me know that he's okay?

Fuck him, and fuck his non-replying attitude. It was never going to be a thing anyway. He'll put his big boy pants on soon enough and we'll be friends again. That's all we can ever be.

I let out a sad and, no doubt, pitiful sigh as I push out my negative feelings. They're not going to help me. I'll wake up in the morning to a brand-new day, these feelings will be gone, and I'll have room for fresh and positive ones.

On that note, maybe I should give myself a little push; see if Nathaniel is up for that coffee sometime soon. It doesn't matter if it goes nowhere, it'll just be nice to have someone in Manhattan who knows me for me.

Fuck it, I'm gonna text him now.

**Me:** Hey, Candy Aisle Guy. It's River  How about that coffee?

I'm sure he won't reply immediately, it's like, one in the morning or some shit. I take a few sips of my water before relaxing back against the bed, my pillows propping me up so the world doesn't keep spinning.

**CAG:** You're up late, everything okay? Coffee sounds great.

The fact that he's replied at this time of the night—or morning... whatever—puts a smile on my face. Asking if I'm okay? Well, that just makes my heart happy. He barely knows me, yet he's checking on me. It's romcom-sweet.

**Me:** I'm a-okay. You don't need to worry about little ol' me. Wanna do coffee now? I probably need ten.

As soon as I press send, I regret it. Why don't cellphones have a drunk detector on them, prohibiting all drunk texts to love interests or sexual exploits forevermore? My phone pings as quickly as it did the first time, and a little excitement actually bubbles in my stomach at what he might've said. I should probably be worried I'm coming off as a bit of a drunken weirdo, but I'm not. I've never felt anything but good vibes from Nathaniel.

**CAG:** Wish I could. How about 1pm? Coco's?

It's short and sweet, but still has me grinning like a hyena on gas. He wishes he could... *Le sigh*.

**Me:** I'll be there with bells on <3

**CAG:** I expect to see at least two *wink emoji* Night, Skittles.

Holy fuck. He just made my drunken wet dreams come true. Well, in theory. If he's given me a nickname, he must like me, right? Coffee was his idea in the first place.

I really need to sleep. I should reply to Nathaniel first, but my eyelids are so heavy I don't think I can. Oh my God, I can close my eyes without everything spinning. I'll just keep them closed for a little longer.

I'll reply soon.

Suffering from a hangover has never been my problem—thank fuck—but losing my inhibitions after a few too many has always been a pain in my ass. Though, I can't really be too mad at drunk me. I managed to bag myself a coffee date with Nathaniel this afternoon, and I'm surprisingly happy about that.

I've tried to avoid making any real connections while living here because it just gets too complicated. My real-life people are in Staten Island. This is just my work playground. After the shit with Kai, I feel like I'm ready. I can totally do this; keep a friendship separate from business.

I can't blame Kai for not always being there for me. We may be best friends, but he has his own life too. He didn't know I needed him a few weeks ago, and it would've been nice to have someone else to turn to other than a client. Tyler is great, but I can't help feeling like letting him in has blurred the lines more than I'm comfortable with.

The universe seems to have sent me Nathaniel at a time when I need it most. Looking over myself in my red, flow-ered skater dress in the mirror, I decide it'll do. I don't want it to look like I'm putting too much effort in here, but I also want to look like I did make an effort. It's a hard life being a woman in this day and age. Forever skating that line of too much or not enough. I'm happy and comfortable with what I'm wearing though, and that's what matters most.

I slip on my heeled Timbs and a cropped denim jack-et before grabbing my purse and heading out to meet Nathaniel. I have no clients booked for this evening, so I'm good to go all day if this goes well.

Christ, I'm an eager beaver today.

Speaking of, it's nice to get ready for a date without having to lube myself up beforehand.

It's mild out today, so the short walk to Coco's is refreshing; it feels great against my flushed skin. I don't know why I'm so nervous... I meet new people all the time. Hell, I piss on people for money for fuck's sake. Yet this little slice of normal has me all aflutter.

Nathaniel's already here as I walk through the doors, a smile gracing his stunning jawline. He looks like freaking Superman, all clean-cut and shiny. *The complete opposite to Kai.* His black Henley top fits snug across his strong shoulders, and his dark hair is swept over to one side in a styled mess. I nod over to him, with a small awkward finger wave, as I make my way to the counter for my favorite coffee.

"What is that monstrosity?" Nathaniel laughs as I place my drink on the tall rounded table and take a seat on the stool next to him, instantly breaking through any anticipated weirdness. Because, yes, my iced café mocha with extra whipped cream, topped with caramel and strawberry sauce does, in fact, look like a monstrosity, but it tastes so good.

"It's the most delicious hangover cure a girl can get." I take a long sip, closing my eyes for a second and just relishing in the taste. When I open them, I smile up at him through my lashes. It's not an intentional Rose move, but I guess she's a part of me, so it's inevitable. "I'm sorry about messaging you at stupid o'clock by the way."

"I didn't mind, I was up. Obviously." He laughs again, and I think I want to bottle it and take it home to release when I feel sad.

"Either way, I'm sorry. What're you drinking?" I'm curious. It's not a coffee, and it doesn't look like something I've seen in here before.

"Strawberry hot chocolate."

"Oh my God, that sounds delicious!"

"Never tasted one? Let's fix that." Pushing his drink in front of me, he encourages me to have a taste.

The flavor that invades my senses as I take a sip is like a little slice of heaven. *Why have I never had one of these before now?*

"Wow, that is something else."

"You should try it with something from the bake case. Did you know they won an award for their pastries?" He slides the menu over for me to take a look.

"Did they?"

"Yeah. They gave a speech to say thanks, said it was a piece of cake." I raise my eyes to peer at him, and he looks so serious, but his face is cracking. There's a smile that wants to break free from his terrible joke-telling skills.

I can't help it. I crack up, causing Nathaniel to lose his cool too.

The next couple of hours pass quickly. We try a few new drinks, sharing them between us so we can sample as many as possible. Turns out, we're both creatures of habit and usually stick to what we know. We've discovered one or two coffees that will never grace our lips again, as well as a few new ones to add to our usual palette.

Sharing a little piece of myself with this man has felt kind of liberating. I've never tried to explain how we grew up surrounded by communal pets to someone before. Nathaniel asks questions and seems really into learning more, keeping me fully at ease the whole time.

"We had, Leaf, Lync, and Lapy, the dogs. And then Limpy and Patches were the cats. I named Patches." I smile at the memory.

"Of course you did. It's the only name that doesn't begin with an L." He lets out one of those sexy, growly laughs again, one that has my insides swirling with need.

It's not that kind of date though, I've realized. Something I'm glad about because this whole thing is lighting up my day.

The gentle touches over the table, soft brushes of the thigh, the occasional "accidental" footsie, are all adding to a growing need I have for this man. But I don't want what I think we could have to be ruined by all that. Not yet anyway. I just want to enjoy this for a little longer. Maybe a few years. When I don't need to work anymore, then it can change.

Fuck. No.

*That's what I've done with Kai. I can't do it to Nathaniel too.*

It's fine. I can do platonic with this man. He clearly wants to go slow anyway. And I don't blame him, considering his wife died of cancer a few years ago. This feels like him just dipping his toes back into the pool. I'm good with that, because I can't offer anything more anyway.

Doesn't mean I can't use him for spank bank material when I get home.

*Mind out of the gutter, River.*

"I wish I could stay longer, but I've got to go. This has been fun." A genuine look of disappointment crosses his face, and I've got to say it makes me feel good about doing this today. I almost backed out, but learning my Candy Aisle Guy is more than just someone pretty to look at has been a success.

My personal cell phone ringing interrupts before I can reply.

"Sorry, I've got to take this."

There's no caller ID when I check. It could be some marketing call but after everything that's happened, I'm not naive enough to believe that. Still, I can't help but answer, an apologetic glance aimed at Nathaniel.

"Hello?"

"You need to be careful, cunt." The voice is computerized and I can't tell who it is, let alone if it's male or female. What it is, though, is creepy as fuck.

"Who is this?"

The line goes dead.

I'm not sure how many minutes pass before Nathaniel speaks, but he pulls me out of whatever fog I've been sucked into.

"River... River? Everything okay?" He's concerned, his brow furrowed as his captivating blue eyes demand an answer.

"Yeah. Must've been a wrong number." I find a little bit of my Rose mask and plaster on a smile, like I didn't just have a mini meltdown. These phone calls are getting out of hand. On my work phone, they were easier to pass off as dickheads just being dickheads. But my personal phone? And they actually spoke this time. It's unnerving to say the least.

How did they even get my personal number anyway? Who the fuck could it be and what is their end game?

"You sure you're okay, gorgeous? You look a little shaken up." The way he speaks to me and calls me gorgeous is almost enough to make me forget. Almost.

"Yeah, thank you." This time, my smile is genuine. It's easy with him. He returns it, a sexy crinkle forming in the corner of his eyes as he does.

"Would you like to join me for dinner sometime?"

"I'd love that."

I appreciate his change of subject. He looks like he wants to ask more about the phone call, but he's holding back.

"Good. Want to walk me out?" As he stands, he holds his arm out for me to slip my hand through. This man has been nothing but the perfect gentleman all afternoon. It's a new experience for me, and I like it a lot.

We exit Coco's together, and it almost feels awkward again as we just stand there and stare at each other. It's like each of us is wondering how best to do this whole goodbye thing.

Nathaniel makes the first move, bringing his hand up to cup the side of my jaw, his fingers on my neck. He leans in and gently kisses the side of my mouth. It's such a friendly move, but it feels so sensual I almost swoon right there.

"Catch ya later, gorgeous." With a lingering smile and a wink, he turns and walks away. Can't say I'm sad about watching him walk away... his jeans hug his tight ass beautifully.

Before I can start my walk home, my work phone pings. It's a text from Tyler.

**Rich One:** Are you free this weekend? My parents are in town. I need you from Friday.

That feels a little personal, the parents, but fuck it. I need to keep myself busy. The heavy-breathing and screaming phone calls are starting to piss me off. Combined with what happened a few weeks ago, I won't lie to myself and pretend I'm not shaken up about it all.

Maybe it's time to re-think my no guns in the apartment rule.

# CHAPTER
# THIRTEEN
## RIVER

Traffic in Manhattan on a Friday night is hit or miss, depending on what's going on or what shows or games are causing chaos. Aaron picks me up at six-thirty p.m. so we can make it to seventy-fifth and Lexington on time for seven.

I check my reflection in my small mirror, tucking a stray strand of hair behind my ear out of nervous habit. I take my job seriously, and showing up pristine for my clients is also in the fucking contract.

Although, truth be told, no one ever mentioned meeting the parents. I don't like it but it's not really the end of the world.

Straightening out my emerald-green skirt, I admire the intricate lace overlay that flows all the way up to the bodice and across my shoulders to form sleeves. Tyler bought it for me on a business trip to Prague a few months back, and I've been waiting for the opportunity to wear it.

"Anything I should know about Tyler's parents? We didn't discuss this so I'm at a loss here." The partition is always down when it's only Aaron and me. It's fun trying to get information out of him. For example, I know he has a nephew and three nieces from two sisters, and a brother who has vowed never to have kids. His family is of Irish descent, his ancestors coming over the Atlantic during the potato famine. I chuckled at the stereotype that is so common here among true New Yorkers.

"I don't know them all that well, but I know Mrs. Walker is a smart cookie and his father doesn't talk much, but he sees everything. Their son takes after them in that respect."

Okay, so that means I need to be on my game. The touching, the lingering gazes like I'm so taken by my handsome boyfriend. I need to play the part of the besotted girlfriend and make him look like the king of the world.

I can do that. Hell, all I need to do is think about the sex and the numerous orgasms he's delivered to make sure my face screams "my hero."

We arrive at the Coq d'Or with five minutes to spare—Tyler standing on the curb, one hand adjusting his tie—giving me a second to put on my game face.

"Okay, Aaron, wish me luck." I take in a deep breath before plastering a smile on my face.

"You'll be perfect, I have no doubt." Sweet man.

When the door opens, Tyler is there, eyes bright, smile wide, extending his hand for me to take. His light gray suit pants and white button-up shirt are snug against his firm body, the shirt open at the top and flashing a little of his sculpted chest. I can't say I hate the view. Helping me out of the car, he gives me a soft kiss on the corner of my mouth and whispers, "You look absolutely stunning."

I grin, and as I air-kiss his cheek, I whisper right back, "I hope so, you paid for this dress."

"That I did and I have zero regrets. Remind me to rip it off of you tonight when we get back to my place."

Well, then. Okay.

"My parents are on the way. Quick update... My mother is Suzannah and my father is David. They're respectively fifty-eight and sixty-two years old. My mother is a cancer survivor, but she loves to talk about it and her charity work. She handed over Astor's Department Stores to me four years ago when her health didn't allow her to continue." He punctuates his words with a deep breath like he's just run a marathon, except he's given me his family history in a nutshell.

"Well, I could have researched all of that on the internet." I tilt my head to his tall frame and smile like I'm the most smitten of all the kittens when I spot a paparazzi fail at being discreet behind the corner of the building.

"Right, how about this..." Tyler wraps my fingers around his bicep and nods his head to the doorman as we both walk into the French restaurant. Reservations here are a bitch to get but I'm not surprised Tyler could get them on such short notice. Hell, I wouldn't be surprised if he had a standing reservation on the weekends. "My mother loves to knit, it's her way of keeping her mind occupied. I used to take her to chemo, and during those long hours she taught me how to knit."

*What the fuck?*

"You knit?" I quirk a brow because, come on. He's a mogul not a homemaker.

"Sure do." His amused grin is aimed straight at me as the waiter takes us to our table and I feel his megawatts straight to my clit.

"Prove it." He laughs at my words, his head thrown back and his face completely relaxed. I'm a little in awe that I made this man—controlled as he is all of the time—drop his walls for a minute.

"I think I have pictures on my phone, I'll show you later." It's my turn to grin because, holy shit, the mental image of this gorgeous billionaire knitting at his mother's side is causing my ovaries to explode.

"Wow, a knitting gazillionaire. Don't see those every day." The mental image is sexy as hell.

"Sorry, I'm only a billionaire, so..." It takes everything in me not to laugh out right. After all, this place is too swanky to lose control.

It's only a few minutes until his parents join our table. We're in Oscar performance mode when they arrive, and I don't know what I expected, but it wasn't what I saw.

Suzannah Astor Walker is the epitome of class and timeless beauty. Her black hair is streaked with gray and swept up into a French twist. The dress she's wearing is stunning, the way the white satin material wraps around her body accentuates her beautiful curves. She looks ten years younger than expected and, in that moment, I hope that I age into even half her stature and class. At her arm is David, and he's sharp but stern faced, like he's got the troubles of the world on his shoulders. Where Suzannah looks young, David's wrinkles map every minute of his sixty-two years. His dark three-piece suit isn't the usual kind of family dinner outfit, but I get the impression he likes to feel important.

"My darling, how are you? I'm so sorry we're late but..." Suzannah kisses Tyler on the cheek. Not an air kiss, but a real peck that leaves a smudge of lipstick, which she wipes away with her thumb. "We saw Issam and his wife Houda—you know our concierge in our building—and they are expecting. Isn't it exciting? A baby!" Oh, God. She has grandmotherly baby fever.

"Yes, of course I remember them." Tyler shakes his father's hand as they murmur words I can't hear because my entire focus is on Suzannah, who has fixed her sights on me. Aaron wasn't kidding. She's sharp and her eagle eyes assess me in two point three seconds. I'm dressed for the part, obviously, and my hair and make-up are on point. Not too much, don't want the mother-in-law to think I'm a whore—oh the irony—but not so little that she could think I'm after his money. This world is too much work, too much calculation and ill-will, for me.

"You must be Rose." She reaches out and clasps my hand in both of hers, looking to Tyler for introductions.

"Mother, this is Rose. Rose, my parents Suzannah and David." I give my most elegant smile and nod my head slightly in deference. Like meeting the fucking queen. It's exhausting.

"It's lovely to meet you, Rose."

"It's an honor, Mrs. and Mr. Walker." Suzannah smiles at Tyler and I know exactly why. Tyler may have omitted giving me information on his parents, but I do my research. Always.

Suzannah Astor inherited the mega department store from her dad back in the day. It was dwindling, too high priced for the ninety's recession, and losing money fast. As soon as she sat in the big chair, she turned the whole company around—starting with the creation of an umbrella company that she named Thunder God Holdings. Instead of downsizing, she invested in up-and-coming fashion designers and basically made them who they are today.

Truth be told, I have a little bit of a lady boner for this woman. So yes, when addressing her and her husband, I chose to start with her, not him as is customary.

"I like her already." I square my shoulders with pride, then have to remind myself that this is all an act. I can't get too attached to this woman because I'm only paid to deceive her.

"Let's sit, shall we?"

We order a bottle of Champagne with our appetizers, talking and laughing, quietly amongst ourselves, of course, and getting to know each other. By this time, I know my fictional card by heart and haven't been taken by surprise at any point in the conversation. Tyler has been the perfect boyfriend. He's attentive and sweet, touching me often and even daring to turn me on under the table. I shut that shit down real fast. I can't concentrate on this façade with his hands all over me.

By our main course, I'm contemplating breaking up with Tyler and marrying his mother. Oh, the scandal. She's witty and sharp, and as large as her presence can be, she seems genuinely interested in what others have to say.

When we order our desserts, I turn to Tyler and excuse myself to the restroom and he bends down to kiss me lightly on the temple.

It's only when I reach the fancy bathroom that I realize Suzannah has followed me. There are two stalls, so I let her choose hers then go to mine. It's awkward, peeing in the same room as your future mother-in-law. No, *fake* future mother-in-law. I cannot forget that.

After washing and drying our hands, Suzannah turns to me and her playful, sweet face morphs into something hard and uncharacteristic.

"Rose, I need to be honest." Well, fuck. This is a plot twist. Dammit, did I fuck up one of my details?

"Um, is everything okay?" I'm legitimately concerned. Tyler's parents cannot know he's hiring a call girl to pretend to be his girlfriend.

"I'm a cancer survivor. You know this, right?" My mind is whirring, trying to go through our earlier conversations and wondering if I offended her somehow.

"Yes, of course. Breast cancer. You beat it about a year later and Tyler took you to chemo." She smiles at that, her love and pride when it comes to her son is palpable.

"Yes, so you also know what can happen because of chemo?" She stands there like a stern school teacher interrogating her underachieving student.

It takes me a second to go through the possible answers. There are two that I can think of off the top of my head.

"The side effects are sickness and hair loss?" My answer sounds more like a question than anything else, but I'm taken aback by her sudden change in demeanor.

"Yes, exactly. Which means, I recognize a wig when I see one." *Fuck*.

My hand automatically reaches for the long red strands of my hair, feeling the heat at my cheeks. Dipping my chin, I smile shyly and tuck it behind my ear.

"I have short hair, it's always been my preference but Tyler was afraid my hairstyle would earn me unpleasant comments in the press or with his entourage. We chose the wig together and I wear it while waiting for my own hair to grow longer." I look back up at her and hope she's appeased. Technically, I'm not lying. Well, except for letting my hair grow out, that's not happening anytime soon.

Suzannah visibly relaxes, like her worries have evaporated with my admission.

"Thank goodness. I was afraid you were trying to pull one over on him." She takes my hand and squeezes. "I'm sorry, I hope you understand."

I squeeze right back. "I do. I promise, Tyler and I are very open and honest with each other." Again, not a lie.

"Good."

"Strip." The elevator to his penthouse hasn't even dinged shut before the order spills from between Tyler's talented lips. "And leave the wig on."

I don't hesitate, my hands at the side of my cocktail dress pulling the hidden zipper down slowly enough to make him clench his teeth with impatience.

"Rose." That one word in that tone says a million things.

*Don't play with me.*

*I call the shots.*

*I need you naked.*

Of course, I follow his lead because this is his game and his fantasies are my command. That's right... it's in the fucking contract.

Speeding up my movements, my dress pooling at my feet in no time, I step out of the puddle and to the side. Tyler's gaze roams my entire form from my heel-clad feet, up the length of my shins, to the tops of my thighs where my garter belt fastens to my stockings. I think he's about to jump on me and fuck me into next year but instead, he walks over to the well-equipped bar and pours two tumblers of fine scotch. The amber liquid sloshes slightly as he brings one glass to me, his eyes never veering from the sight of my half naked body.

"You were perfect tonight." I curtsy like he's my king and I'm his servant. I suppose I would be if we were in the Middle Ages in Europe. I'd be his mistress or his whore.

Fuck, that's exactly what I am, but at least in this scenario I'm getting paid enough to live comfortably.

I take his offering, and we clink our glasses together before we each take a sip. Our eyes are locked over the rims and I watch, rapt, as he knocks back the contents and waits for me to hand over my glass. I'm not courageous enough to drink the whole thing in one go, so I take a sip and wince at the burn down my throat.

I don't think I'd be a great addition to the lifestyle of the rich and famous. I imagine they all sit around counting their dollar bills, drinking from bottles of liquor that could be used as a down payment on a house, and smoking cigars from embargoed countries. I prefer sitting around a fire, drinking wine and smoking a joint.

Tom-Ay-to, tom-Ah-to.

He places the tumblers on the counter then slowly makes his way back to me—unhooking one cufflink, then the other—and stops a mere two inches to my front.

"My parents liked you." His words are soft, almost a whisper, as he brings the back of his fingers to my neck before sliding across my collarbone and over to my shoulder. His eyes are following his own movements, like he's in a trance as he watches his skin caress my own.

I'm not impatient or twitchy. I let him do what he needs to do. This is his show, I follow his lead, always.

"I'm glad to hear it." Although, what I want to say is that he's playing a dangerous game, and getting his parents to love me is only going to raise unwanted questions when we inevitably "break-up."

And it *is* inevitable.

One day, he's going to find someone who will not only get his dick harder than stone but make his heart melt like heated butter.

"Are you?" His gaze is on mine now and he's sincere, he really wants to know.

"Why wouldn't I be?" My question is left unanswered as he hums to himself before resuming the light perusal of his fingers over my heating flesh. I don't push him, I don't repeat myself. I let him contemplate whatever it is he's stuck on. Something is clearly on his mind; maybe he's regretting the show we put on. Maybe he's wondering if it's time for him to truly move on from the pain his ex-wife caused him.

I want to tell him that she didn't deserve him, never did. He's a kind, attentive man who works hard to provide for his family, and she was a selfish bitch who, instead of speaking with him, decided she wanted to fuck his best friend.

Oh, how that story sounds familiar to me.

My attention is back on him as my strapless bra is ripped right off my body in one strong pull from his fingers. What's left of it thrown to the side, landing on the back of the couch.

Both of his hands are cupping my tits, his thumbs rubbing circles over my nipples before he leans in and sucks one into his mouth, then the other. I gasp at the warm feel, and the tinge of pain as his teeth graze the tender skin shoots a jolt of pleasure through my body before he releases me, exposing my wet flesh to the ambient temperature.

It's warm in his penthouse, but his mouth is scorching hot.

"Do you know what I see when I look at you?" The number of different answers to that question are too many to count.

*A whore.*

*A lost soul.*

*A heartless business woman.*

When I don't answer—I'm pretty sure his question was rhetorical anyway—he continues, shocking me with his revelation.

"A smart, beautiful woman who has so much to give but refuses to see herself as anything other than what she pretends to be." I'm frozen in surprise. Why would he say that?

I don't have time to deny or argue or any of the hundreds of things I should have said to him because he's suddenly on his knees, unfastening the garters—they're just for show anyway—and sliding them down along with my silk panties. I'm left in only my stockings and heels as he sweeps me up in his arms and walks me to his bedroom, like we're newlyweds fucking for the first time after exchanging vows.

Everything about this is strange, unfamiliar. Where's the dominant sex god? Where are the restraints and the butt plugs? Where are his salacious orders?

Depositing me on his huge four-poster bed, he stands at the foot of it and begins undressing. Everything he does is infuriatingly slow. He removes one piece of clothing at a time, all the while watching me with his hungry gaze. The tie is first, sliding off from around his neck and dropping to the bench. Then he pops each of the buttons on his shirt, one after the other, until his hard, defined chest is exposed to my sight. Shrugging off the fabric, he places it next to his tie and starts unfastening his dress pants. The button, then the zipper, until they fall down the length of his long, powerful legs.

He's commando, of course. He always is, it seems.

The spring of his thick cock greets me like an angry soldier ready for battle. It reaches the line of his navel, precum already beading at the slope of its head like a beacon to my mouth.

Without a conscious thought, I lick my lips like I'm starving for him, for his cock, for the feeling of control while I suck him down my throat. I'm thankful when his gaze zeroes in on my movement and understanding shines in his eyes.

"You hungry for my dick, Rose? You want me to fuck your face like a good little girl?" Goddamn, I'm a sucker for dirty talk.

I don't answer with words, instead I scramble to a sitting position before sliding down to my knees, mouth open wide, hands on my thighs, and wait for him to feed me.

His top teeth sink into his bottom lip and I swear I can practically feel the excitement rolling off his body. One hand is now at his cock, stroking, pulling, thumb gliding across his precum as he watches me watching him.

"You are fucking perfect." With one step, he's erased the remaining space between us as his hand flies to the nape of my neck and his thumb pushes hard into the junction at my jaw, ordering me to open wider.

I do as I'm told and with our eyes boring into each other, he thrusts his cock into my mouth. Tyler grunts as I take him in and suck him deep to the back of my throat, humming when I feel him reach my gag reflex. I know how to do this, I've had enough practice to manage any size or depth.

I've also learned that clients love to feel powerful while their dicks are buried in a woman's willing mouth, especially if they are capable of making them cry from the act. I'm not pretending with Tyler. His cock is long and thick and impossible to swallow whole but he's a man like any other. When the head of his dick bumps against my throat, demanding I open up for him, I feel my gag tears well-up and slide down my cheeks.

The look of utter satisfaction on his face is fucking priceless. He's proud of me. Of himself. Of this. He's fucking turned on watching my body react to his thrusting.

"You're fucking gorgeous with my dick filling your mouth, you know that?" He pulls out and grabs at my nape as he slams back inside me, going impossibly deeper, making my tears fall faster. "Your tears are fucking beautiful, smearing your make-up and making you all dirty for me." Jesus fuck, I'm so turned on right now I have to squeeze my thighs to avoid slapping my hand to my clit and getting myself off.

Tyler's eyes dart from my gaze to my mouth and back again, his hips accelerating, his grip tightening. It's like he's possessed; his body tense, his jaw clenched as he fucks my mouth in and out. In and out. My tears falling, his dick pistoning until he stops it all and lifts me to my feet. Suddenly, his mouth is on mine and he's kissing me with a violence I've never felt from him before. Like he's communicating unsaid words he's never confessed before.

Like he's telling me secrets I don't want to hear.

Our mouths dance frantically, our tongues dueling, teeth clashing, and I'm suddenly in his arms, my legs wrapped around his waist as my heels fall to the floor—one then the other. It's only when I'm on his mattress that he reaches up to the night stand and, mere seconds later, sheathes himself with a condom and slides inside me.

I'm so fucking wet for him, there's no resistance. No need to get used to him.

In our frenzy, I expect him to fuck me hard and fast, making us both come in mere minutes. But Tyler surprises the fuck out of me when he slows down, almost to a full stop. Balancing his weight on his forearms, he cages me in, looking at me as he leisurely pushes in and out of my all-too-greedy pussy.

"Take off your wig."

I must look confused but it only brings a bright, almost boyish grin to his face.

"I don't want to end this. I want to see you, the real you." I smile back up at him and snort, the noise so unladylike I almost apologize.

"I've seen you get hard mere minutes after coming, Tyler. I'm not worried this will end too quickly." I'm purposefully being obtuse to the wig comment. And that's when I see it.

The shift.

The change from billionaire client to vulnerable man. It scares the fuck out of me because I can deal with all sorts of men in my bed, but this? I'm not used to this. Not even with Kai.

"I don't want this to end," he repeats, changing up his statement so that it means so much more than it did before.

His groin grinds into my clit, making me jump and causing my hips to dart off the bed and closer to him. "Oh God, that feels so good." I need to concentrate on the orgasm that he's building up for me. Need to make sure we keep this to sex and not stray into uncharted territory.

"Rose," he whispers my name like a prayer as he begins fucking me harder and harder. His tone is so at odds with the filthy movement of his hips, of his thighs, of his cock now slamming in and out of my dripping wet pussy.

"Stay with me." My back arches as he brings his mouth down to mine and kisses me, not with want, but with need. With adoration and respect. He's fucking me like his whore and kissing me like his lover.

I'm so confused, but the sexed-up part of my brain is choosing to ignore anything beyond the impending climax I feel rising from that erect bundle of nerves to my core, to my stomach. I scream into Tyler's mouth as he plunges one last time inside me before stilling and grinding, emptying his seed into the condom.

"Fuck, Rose. We're perfect together."

Nope, not my imagination.

Panting and struggling to breathe, he stays buried inside me as he secures the rubber at the base and pulls out carefully, discarding it into the trash next to his bed.

Then his attention is right back on me, his eyes as intense as ever.

"I want to take care of you. I want to be everything to you. Because, Rose, I swear to fuck, you are perfect for me."

I reach up and kiss his mouth tenderly before promptly nipping this conversation in the bud.

"It's not even my real name. I'm not perfect for you, Tyler. I'm just really fucking good at my job." He recoils at my words. The shock on his face breaking my heart as I take the opportunity to gently push him away and slip out from under him.

I can't let him create this neatly wrapped image in his mind of a Julia Roberts and Richard Gere getting a happily ever after. It's not happening. Not now, at least, and not with him.

I have to end this. It's a shame, though. I really fucking loved the orgasms he gave me.

Looking over my shoulder as I pad off into the bathroom, I give him my final blow.

"Can you call Aaron and have him take me home, please?"

# CHAPTER FOURTEEN

## RIVER

The car ride home was tense. Aaron's a perceptive man and he knew something was up. Yet, he remained the loyal driver that he is and didn't say a word.

What happened last night with Tyler is something I'd never expected from him. He's always so in control of himself and his emotions. Working with him is something I'm going to miss, but I can't have clients catching feelings. That's unfair to everyone involved.

I suppose it just goes to show how caught up we were in our roles, which makes me feel like shit for allowing him to think this could be real. But we knew what this was from the start; we have a fucking contract for Christ's sake. I guess that's null and void now though.

*Argh*! Men make me so mad. Why do they have to be such complicated creatures?

He had disappeared to fuck knows where by the time I came out of the bathroom and gathered my things. It feels like we left this thing unfinished, but I needed to make my boundaries clear. I'll give him a few days before I call to officially end our contract.

Fuck it, I'm going to roll myself a doob. These are extenuating circumstances and I need to chill the fuck out. I don't need drunk me contacting Kai or Nathaniel right now. I've already thought about both, so wine isn't the best choice tonight.

Sitting by the window, I watch as my smoke-circles evaporate into the cool night air. Floating up to the dark sky, they swirl and twist, and they're free.

To be that free would be a wonderful thing.

Free from responsibilities.

Free from worries.

Free from feeling so stuck in the life I've created for myself. The complications arising from my chosen lifestyle sometimes feel too great.

But those are the thoughts of a quitter, and a quitter I am not.

This is just another one of those blips. I'll allow myself to wallow in the whole Tyler thing for tonight, but tomorrow is a fresh new day.

Noise from the street below catches my attention and my eyes grow wide as I watch Tyler speaking to Mr. Bobby, moving his arms in an animated way. I can't make out what he's saying, but whatever it is, is likely to end up with Tyler in my apartment.

Before I can look away, Tyler's penetrating gaze meets mine. He then turns and waltzes right into my building.

*Fuck.*

Well, I'm not getting changed for him. This is my apartment, my space, and my time. He's not paying for this, so my old Nine Inch Nails band tee—once my dad's—and sky-blue Elsa boy shorts will have to do. It's eleven at night for fuck's sake. Most normal people are getting ready for bed. I hope that's not what he's here for. It was hard enough seeing his face crumble last night.

Padding over to the front door, warm bed socks on my feet, I open it, ready for his inevitable arrival. After turning the coffee machine on, I take a seat at the breakfast bar. This isn't a sit-on-the-comfortable-sofa kind of conversation.

"Rose." Just one word is all it takes to bring a lump to my throat. The word is full of hurt and confusion, and there's nothing I can really do to make that any better.

"Hi, Tyler. Coffee?"

"Why is your apartment door wide open? This is Manhattan. Anyone could just walk in."

"And here you are." I raise an eyebrow at him as I pour two cups of coffee.

"Fine. We need to talk about last night."

"I don't know what you're expecting from me, but I can't give you what you need anymore. I can't be that girl for you, I'm sorry."

Sliding his coffee over to him as he stands at the end of my breakfast bar, I fidget with the handle of my own cup in front of me.

The crushed expression on his handsome face doesn't make this easy.

"In another life, we'd be amazing together. You're a fucking fantastic guy, and some day you're going to find the perfect woman for you."

It's unnerving seeing this successful, confident business mogul affected in this way. He's lost some of his spark and I don't like it. I should be flattered knowing a man like him could see a future with a woman like me, but I feel shitty for being the cause of his pain.

Combing his fingers through his already-ruffled hair, Tyler looks defeated.

"I don't even fucking know why I came here or what I expected, but I'll be honest, I didn't think you'd turn me down again."

"Sorry?" My awkward apology helps a slither of a smile appear on the corner of his beautiful mouth.

*I'm really going to miss that mouth.*

"People don't usually say no to me, Rose..." With his head dipped down, he's looking at me through his lashes, almost apologetically. "But I get it. I'm sorry I pushed it too far."

Although I'm not surprised, I'm still relieved he's not being a douche about this.

He sits on the stool beside me, making sure to give me my personal space. Something I know is difficult for him to do.

Coffee cup in hand, I gently nudge his arm with my shoulder so he looks at me before I speak.

"You don't need to be sorry, Ty. We just got swept up in the act. And now it's time to move on. Can I be real with you for a moment?" I look at him expectantly, waiting for him to answer.

"Sure." He gives me a resigned smile, knowing this isn't going to be what he wants to hear.

Taking a deep breath, I prepare myself for a quick story time. Hopefully this will help Tyler move on easier.

"You're a sexy, intelligent, overall amazing guy. Any girl would be lucky to have you. You're attentive and a fantastic lover, and if life were any different, you'd be perfect for me. But it's not. Truth is, I've been in love with someone for my entire life. My heart is already full, and it wouldn't be fair for me to pretend otherwise." I sip my coffee when I'm finished, glancing at him over the rim, reminding me of the way he looked at me last night.

"That's not what I was expecting."

"And my name isn't Rose, but you knew that already."

His grin is wider now, there's still some sadness in his eyes, but that will heal with time. I'm not his end-game girl. Whoever that is, will be a very lucky lady indeed.

"Fuck, I feel like such an idiot for showing up here." He rubs the back of his neck with one palm. "Guess I better call Aaron to come and pick me up."

Agreeing to Nathaniel's dinner invitation this evening probably wasn't my best move, but after all the drama with

Tyler the last couple of nights, it'll be nice to have a normal conversation.

Kai still isn't replying to my texts.

The little Mom-and-Pop diner we're in is perfect for a Sunday evening. Warm, home-cooked food and lots of coffee is exactly what I need. It's like Nathaniel had a sixth sense when he texted me this morning to join him. As if he knew I needed a little slice of normal.

"May I take your order?" The waiter looks young, probably the owners' son.

"Yeah, can I get a triple cheeseburger with everything, loaded chili fries, and a strawberry milkshake, please?"

*Mmm*, Nathaniel's order sounds good.

"I'll have the same, please, and a refill on my coffee. Thank you."

Nathaniel's face is almost comical as the waiter scribbles on his notepad.

"Is that everything?"

"Is that everything, River?" His raised eyebrow and amused grin tell me he's surprised at the amount of food I've ordered. My reply is a raised eyebrow of my own and a nod of my head. "That's all, thank you."

With the waiter gone, we're alone in our cozy little booth again. I know I've thought it before, but if Clark Kent were real, Nathaniel would be him. Minus the glasses. He's wearing a light-gray sweater, which accentuates his chest and biceps beautifully, and his hair is styled in its usual swept over mess. I could stare at this man and his smile forever.

"What made you choose this place?" What was supposed to be a simple question feels like so much more as I see that sadness flash through Nathaniel's eyes. He clears his throat before answering, as if he's deciding what he's going to say.

"Honestly, my wife and I used to come to places like this all the time. They were her favorite. She said they always reminded her of good, old-fashioned dates. Shit. I just made this weird, didn't I?" The way he looks at me with such honesty and sadness almost breaks my heart for him. But it's also another excellent reminder of what this is. A friendship. Nothing more. Neither of us are in a position to take things any further, and I'm okay with that.

"Not weird at all. It's okay if you want to talk about her, you know? No judgment or weirdness from me. Okay?" I'm just laying it out there, because if I want a new friend—as fuckable as he is—then I have to make the effort.

Also, shyness is cute on him.

By the time we get to dessert, I swear my eyes are bigger than my belly. The half-eaten apple pie and ice-cream in front of me is my nemesis at this moment.

"Oh my God, I think I'm having a food baby." Leaning back on the red and white bench seat, I rub my full stomach. Again, that sadness in Nathaniel's eyes comes back. I place my hand on his and squeeze lightly as I speak in almost a whisper. "Do I remind you of her?"

Bringing my fingers to his mouth, he kisses them gently, a sad smile on his lips, and that's all the answer I get. I'm not going to push for more. This is obviously difficult for him and what he's shared so far feels like a gift.

"I also need a food nap. You know, when you eat so much that it makes you drowsy enough to sleep for a week? But..." I lean in as if I'm about to spill my deepest, darkest secret. "If you sleep too long, then you miss out on bed time snacks. And we can't have that."

He leans in, and our mouths are so close. *So close.* But he doesn't kiss me. His lips quirk in that gorgeous smile of his, the corners of his eyes crinkling mischievously.

"No, we definitely can't have that." He clears his throat and leans back, like maybe this just got too intense.

"We should get you home then, Sleeping Beauty, before you turn into a pumpkin."

Oh bless this sweet man. But he cracks me up.

"Cinderella was the one with the pumpkin, Sleeping Beauty was the one with the spinning wheel."

He chuckles, and I shrug my shoulders like I'm an expert on Disney princesses.

"Well, I'll make sure to remember that for next time."

"Next time? That's a little presumptuous, don't you think?" I'm kidding, and he knows it.

"Some people say it's my best quality."

I can definitely think of some better qualities about this man than being presumptuous.

Outside the diner, Nathaniel waits with me until my Uber arrives, his arms around me from behind to keep the chill off. I forgot my jacket and the off-the-shoulder top I'm wearing isn't really fall attire. His hard chest is against my back, his warm breath against my neck, and I can't help the feeling of contentment that washes over me.

My car pulls up and I let my driver, Eric, know I'll just be a second. Turning to Nathaniel, I wrap my arms around his waist rather than tiptoeing to reach his neck. He envelops me in his embrace, like the best kind of bear-hug one can experience. As I pull away, he grabs the side of my face, the same possessive way he did before, his fingers caressing my neck. Then he leans in and places a soft kiss on the side of my mouth, barely brushing against my lips.

"Sleep well, Skittles."

"Night, Nathaniel."

"Call me Nate." He gives me his signature wink before turning to the car and leaning inside the front passenger window. "Make sure she gets home safely." Taking his cellphone in hand, he holds it up and snaps a picture of Eric. "Just in case, man. Just in case."

He watches as I get in the car and reminds me to put my seatbelt on, then continues to stand there and watch as we drive away.

My apartment is warm when I arrive home, just how I like it this time of year. My adrenaline is high on some kind of cheesy happiness as I float around getting ready for bed. It was so nice to just have a simple connection with someone. A boy and a girl, no money exchanges, no unhealthy baggage.

A knock on my front door brings me out of my own head. It's almost midnight, why would anyone be knocking on my door this late?

The last person to show up at my door at this time of night was Tyler, but I'm sure it can't be him.

Peering through my peephole, I see no one. I can hear pounding down the stairs, so I run to the window to see if I can catch whoever it was as they leave. Fat chance, the light across the street is out so I can't see anything but shadows.

So weird.

I peer through my peephole once more, ignoring the niggling feeling in my belly warning me something is wrong here. When I see no one is out there, I open the door anyway.

A package wrapped in some kind of black silk and tied with a black satin ribbon sits on my doormat. Why is there a package? It's not my birthday until March, Christmas isn't for another few months, so why is someone leaving an anonymous present for me?

There's a card poking out of the top, so I bend to pick it up.

*I thought this would make you feel better.*

*You need to be more careful.*

What the fuck?

Opening the present cautiously, I have no idea what it is or who it's from. What I *do* know is there's a strange smell coming from inside.

Oh my fucking God!

No!

It can't...

I'm going to puke. Luckily, I make it to the bathroom on time.

Some sick bastard has sent me a motherfucking dick and balls. A *decaying* dick and balls.

A decaying dick and balls that look pretty familiar, reminding me of one dumpling-dicked asshole.

Everything I ate this evening is now in the bottom of the toilet, and I'm pissed. For many, many reasons.

One of them being that some motherfucking sicko knows where I live.

Jesus, this is all too much.

Kai, Tyler, the fucking weirdo a few weeks ago, the anonymous phone calls... and now this?

Fuck.

I'm spiraling and I don't know how to stop it as my anger and anxiety get the best of me. Tears spring from my eyes and stream down my cheeks. My breaths are heavy as I allow myself to break down. I need to get out of here.

I need Kai.

# Chapter Fifteen

## River

When I have downtime, I like to watch Netflix. More specifically, I love watching anything crime related. *Luther, Dexter, The Irishman,* it doesn't matter. If it's a mind-fuck puzzle, I'll watch it. And if it's True Crime, even better.

One thing I have never been able to understand is why victims are always seen with a blanket or shawl over their shoulders as they explain to the police what happened. Even in the summer.

It's not until I'm sitting on my kitchen stool with a goddamn fleece blanket wrapped around me that I get it. Fear makes your extremities run cold. Wrapping something around your upper body helps with that and also makes you feel safe.

And that's what I need. To feel safe.

My first phone call after receiving a literal dick in a box was to Kai. It went to voicemail after only one ring, which means he saw my name flashing on the screen and made the conscious choice to hang up on me.

I'd be enraged if I weren't so fucking devastated.

My second phone call was to three-one-one—the number in New York City for non-emergencies. I didn't feel a call to nine-one-one was warranted seeing as the danger wasn't exactly imminent.

"Jesus Christ," were the first two words the male police officer muttered when he opened the box. I think he grabbed his junk on reflex to make sure it was all still there. "That SNL skit is much funnier than this shit."

The female officer wasn't impressed. *I feel ya, sister.*

"Do you have any idea who could have sent you this?" I was expecting this question. It makes perfect sense to want to narrow down the list of possible suspects. Honestly, I couldn't see any of my clients sending me anything, never mind a penis with its balls neatly placed underneath.

I shudder at the mental image that I probably will never be able to erase. The world doesn't have enough bleach for this.

"No. I'm a life coach, my clients don't know where I live since I go to them. My life is pretty limited as far as acquaintances are concerned." Officer Nunez is jotting everything down on her phone and it goes against everything I've seen on television.

Aren't they supposed to carry spiral note pads? I'm staring at her phone and wondering if she's actually typing out a text message to her husband, telling him she's got a fun case to talk about at breakfast in the morning.

"Miss?" I blink up at the officer who's staring at me expectantly.

"I'm sorry, yes?"

"Besides this..." She pauses, probably trying to find a better expression than *dick in a box,* and comes up with, "...unconventional gift, has anything else happened? Any other incidents that could help us?" The phone calls, the masked voices, the weird breathing. But fuck. I can't tell her about the attack. How in the hell would I explain that? I have no name, no police report, and most of all, I'm a fucking prostitute. I doubt that little tidbit is going to please the officer.

"I've had a few calls, some of them freaked me out a little so I reported those to the police as well." She continues taking notes, nodding like she approves of my leaving a trail for them to pick up.

"With our precinct? Sometimes communication is... difficult if the report is elsewhere." Translation, paperwork doesn't travel from one station to the other. I get it.

"Yes and it was... um, two months ago? Middle of August sometime. I'm sorry, I can't remember the exact date but I have the report here somewhere." I go to stand but she places a warm hand on my shoulder, looking me straight in the eyes with a kind of reassuring smile that brings some of the much needed warmth back into my hands and toes.

"You're fine, don't worry."

"No one actually touched the severed, um, penis, right?" The male officer looks uncomfortable as he asks me the question. Just the thought of touching any of that sends a cold chill running down my spine.

"No. God, no." I don't know if he actually hears me because Officer Nunez repeats my answer a little louder for him.

"River, are you all right?" Mr. Bobby is at the door and as soon as I see him, I cry like a child who's in need of a comforting hug. "Oh, sweet girl. Hold on, now. Let me get to you." With difficulty, he makes it to my side and engulfs me in his embrace, holding me close and rocking me like a baby.

"And you are?" I don't see Officer Nunez, but I hear her tone. Suspicion. It jars my memories of the shows I like to watch, and I'm guessing she's thinking the same thing I am.

It's always those closest to you.

Also, criminals like to return to the scene of the crime, acting like the good Samaritan.

Except Mr. Bobby is almost eighty years old and despite his big frame, I doubt he'd have the force or the will to hold down some dude while he cut off his dick.

Also, it would make absolutely no sense.

"I'll be okay, Mr. Bobby. Just some random person playing a prank, I think. Officer Nunez, this is..." It's then I realize I don't know his full name. Everyone in the neighborhood just calls him Mr. Bobby. Thankfully, he intervenes.

"Robert McGraw. I live downstairs, I'm the super of this building."

The whole thing took forever. Between the questions, the forensics, more questions, it was exhausting and all I really wanted was for them to leave. Once they were finally gone, the apartment fell eerily silent. Mr. Bobby stayed behind, as if he knew I needed the comfort.

"When did this happen?" Mr. Bobby looks frazzled, like he's somehow responsible for any of this. "I locked the access door at eight tonight when I went back to my place."

I sigh because that's the thing. You need a code to get in downstairs, so either it's someone in the building or... I have no fucking clue.

Robotically, I repeat my story to Mr. Bobby, too tired to put any emotion into it.

"You shouldn't stay here alone tonight. Is there anyone who could come get you? Anyone you could stay with?" I stare at my kind neighbor and there's only one name that pops into my head.

*Kai.*

I try again, hoping and silently praying that he'll answer. Except it's almost one-thirty in the morning and Kai works at seven, so my expectations are quite low.

Straight to voicemail this time. His phone is off and I'm fucked.

I try the next best thing.

He answers on the fourth ring.

"What the fuck, River, it's...fuck. What time is it?" I hear rustling and then Petal's voice answering him. It takes a minute, but concern is clear in his voice.

"Are you okay? Did something happen?" I don't like to play victim on any day and definitely not when it comes to Everest. I'm the adult. He should be completely worry free when it comes to me. I'm the big sister, but right now, I just need my family.

"I'm fine but something did happen. Is it okay if I come to your place right now? I have a key so no need to get up. I'll just crash on your couch." There's silence for a little while. I'm guessing Everest is in shock because I never ask for help. If I had another option, I wouldn't be asking now either.

I thought about Nathaniel, but good grief, one dinner does not equate white knight. I'm not ready to scare him off that quickly.

"Of course, River. You know our home is your home. I'm just worried, that's all." Bless his heart because it literally *is* in my name.

"I know and I'll explain it all in the morning. Go back to sleep, I'll be fine." I smile because Everest is my favorite teddy bear.

"I'll come pick you up at the ferry, I don't like you taking a car at this time of night. I don't like you being so far away right now either." I sigh. I need to choose my battles, and telling him not to come is only going to create an unnecessary argument.

"Fine. Okay. Thank you. I'll text you my arrival time."

It was almost three in the morning when I arrived at their house. I've left fear behind and now, as I lie on my brother's couch, the anger is taking precedence.

Who the fuck thinks dropping off a dick on my doorstep is a good idea for a gift?

I can't think of a single person who would do that. Not a one.

Just from the note alone, it didn't sound like a threat. There was no real malice in the words either. The guy—an assumption on my part, but shit—sounded like he was happy to do this for me.

But why?

"Morning, River. Come here, give me a hug." Worried Petal is up and her need to comfort me is overwhelming.

"Oh my God, I'm fine. Actually, I'm pissed now." I don't miss Petal's quirk at the corner of her mouth. I think I amuse her. Just when I'm about to ask her what she's got planned for today, my brother comes barreling down the stairs.

"Fuck, man. I'm running late. I still need to load up the van with the produce." He's pulling on his beanie, the five Grateful Dead bears dancing in a circle. My chest warms at the sight because it was our dad's, and every winter since their deaths, Everest has worn it without fault.

"I can help!" I jump out of Petal's arms after giving her a small squeeze and put on my shoes.

"Dude, it's fucking freezing outside. Don't worry about it, okay? Stay inside with Petal and maybe help her with her soaps?" The smile he gives his wife is nothing short of adoring.

"You go on, my love. River and I will get all of our chores done. I made you something to eat. It's in your lunch box." They kiss, more than once, before reluctantly pulling away from each other.

Their uninhibited show of affection is almost disgusting, but that's just jealousy talking.

By the time we eat and get all the soap ingredients ready, I've told Petal the entire sordid story about last night.

"You should send an email to Justin Timberlake's team and tell them you're a victim of a dick in a box incident." I stop and look at her in shock.

"Now, how in the hell do you know anything about JT? I thought you were only into the sixty's icons." Petal's cheeks turn a cute little shade of pink as she shoots me a side-eye.

"A girl needs her secrets and he's it. I mean, I love Bob Dylan but he's not fantasy material anymore." I laugh, but then my mind goes straight to sex and all the fucked up shit I'm used to seeing. Which has me wondering if Petal has any kinks. And that's when my brain comes to a screeching halt. I absolutely do not want to know if she and my brother like a little freak under the sheets.

"So, the trick is to make sure you use a stainless-steel pitcher for the lye. Plastic is okay, but I'd rather do away with anything made from crude oil. Definitely no aluminum. The lye mixed with the water will dissolve it and then we'll die from too much hydrogen in the air. Your brother wouldn't approve." She chuckles and hands me all the safety equipment I need to put on as she mixes the ingredients.

I've been so far removed from my roots that I've completely forgotten how to do all of these things. Make soap, make my own bread from scratch. The artistic fiber in my being that my mother loved to nurture has been pretty much dormant these last few years.

I suppose I have other things on my mind and sitting around singing *Kumbaya* isn't on my priority list. I know I'm being a bitch—simple living is actually a lot of work—but I'm afraid that if I stop and evaluate my life, I'll want to go back in time.

I have come to grips with the fact that I love my "things" and downsizing isn't on my radar. That said, I live in one of the most expensive cities in the world where real estate is gold and fitting large things in small spaces is its own form of art.

"Fuck!" I almost drop the lye mixture, my gloves not thick enough to sustain the natural heat it produces.

"Oh, no. I forgot to remind you it gets hot. Are you okay?" We're talking with masks on and I can barely understand her soft voice. Her big brown eyes tell me everything I need to know. She's worried.

These two are going to be amazing parents one day. Just like our parents.

The exact opposite of me.

"It's okay, it mostly surprised me. It's funny the things you forget even though you've done them a thousand times. Mom used to make soaps for us. We never sold them, but it was shared with those living on our land."

"You never talk about your parents." It's not an accusation, Petal doesn't judge or look down on people, she's just making an observation and she's not wrong. Talking about them hurts. Talking about them reminds me of why they're dead. Why I have to do everything I can to make sure I make it up to Everest, who had to grow up without parents. I don't answer her as she hands me another stainless-steel container and we begin mixing the oils.

"Wait, you're not using coconut oil?" My mother loved the smell and the feel of it.

"Not for this batch. I wanted to try the babassu oil, I read about its antioxidant properties." She places the lye on the side and sets the timer for forty minutes. "Stop changing the subject, River. You and I both know you don't really care what's happening with the soap." I start to argue with her but she arches a brow and dares me to contradict her.

We don't lie to each other. Well, that's the story, anyway. Everything in my life is a lie as far as they are concerned. I refuse to burst the bubble around their happy lives.

"Fine. Let's do this. You have until that timer goes off to ask your questions." Petal's mouth opens but I stop her with my hand, palm facing her, in the universal sign for hold on. "I reserve the right to use as many jokers as I wish."

"Well that's not fair." Her little pout is cute but it won't deter me.

"Fine. First question. What the hell is this story about you and the rich guy?" I frown because I was not expecting this one. I should have, but since our contract is null and void, I've put him at the back of my mind.

Running a hand through my short hair, I sigh then meet her gaze. "I broke it off Friday night."

Her face lights up like a fucking Fourth of July celebration as she kneels on the carpeted floor and brings her steepled hands to her mouth. "Oh my Gods, this means you and Kai—"

"Stop right there." Again with the palm to face. "We are not doing the Kai talk. I need to have a serious sit-down conversation with him first and if anything comes of it, we'll keep you in the loop."

Once the Kai subject is put to rest we chat about Manhattan, how expensive everything is getting, and I tell her about my "life coaching" job.

"I think it's neat that you teach people how to release stress, take in the positive and expel the negative. I truly believe if we can all do this it will bring us true peace one day." Oh, to be young and full of dreams.

"Maybe." Who am I to burst her bubble? I mean, I didn't technically lie to her. Officially, that's my job and I pay taxes on said life lessons. I do teach men how to relax and expel their negativity through the form of really powerful orgasms.

Which reminds me that I have a new client and this guy is going to be full of unexpected kink. Who knows? Maybe it'll be fun.

The rest of the day is spent finishing the batch of soap that will now sit for about six weeks. Then we took a long walk in Allison Park. We brought our yoga mats for a little relaxation and sat for a bit of meditation.

I honestly had fun today, centering and truly listening to my "self" gave me the perspective and courage to face some of my demons. I think I even found a beginning of forgiveness or understanding when it comes to Kai and Freya.

Most importantly, I decided it was time to be completely honest with Kai. Time to come clean and admit my feelings, which he *has* to already know, and tell him I'm ready. I'll even talk about my job and we can figure out a way to make it work. I could truly become a life coach. In fact, I could do anything I want with him by my side.

We return home just as the sun begins to set and I feel a new purpose in my very core. My belly flutters when we reach their street and Kai's truck comes into view.

He's here.

Fuck, I'm nervous.

What if he's still mad? What if he doesn't feel the same?

What if—

No. I refuse to question my decision. I've done my soul-searching and I am ready. Kai and I are like the moon and the sun, never in the same place at the same time, but tonight, we will meet in the middle, for our own private eclipse.

"Kai's here, hope that's okay…" Petal speaks softly as though she's afraid to disrupt this moment. Or maybe she's afraid I'll bolt.

"No, it's great. We should talk anyway." I grin at the prospect and by the time I reach the front door and hear my brother's booming voice, I'm already running into the living room and about to declare my love for Kai.

"Hey! I wan—" My feet freeze at the entrance, the sight in front of me making my heart sink like a plane going down before it crashes and burns.

It's not Kai I see first.

It's Freya. All smiles and tears and fire and her eyes. My gaze darts to Everest, who's handing Kai a beer and a glass of home-made bubbly to Freya. I know it's homemade because Petal explained the process to me today while we made soap.

Then my gaze lands on Kai and we just stare. At first, his honey irises dare me to say something. A split second later, all I can see is a wall that makes every single resolution from today crumble like a house of cards.

"Oh! Hello." Petal is as surprised as I am, except she moves past me and wraps an arm around Everest. I'm too chicken shit to walk all the way in so I just stand at the archway like a fucking creeper.

"River, we didn't think you'd be here." I want to remind Freya that technically this is my house so she can fucking shut her mouth, but then I think of my parents, who believed anger was the vessel of hurt, so I push it all down and smile. Also like a creeper.

"Some fucked up shit happened last night, so she's staying with us for a bit." Everest, ever the poet.

Kai's eyes dart immediately to me, the concern there, then gone. It's like he's actively trying not to feel anything. Dammit, he's still mad about Tyler. I'll explain later when Freya is gone.

"Oh, well, maybe the news will cheer you up, then." Freya is practically holding herself back from yelling, her excitement a little too potent for my tired mind. I am hoping she just got a job clear across the fucking country. I hear California's nice all year round.

Crossing my arms and leaning against the wall, I look straight at Kai and wait for whatever it is that's so amazing that she had to come over tonight to announce it.

I think my body knows before my mind can even catch up. It's the setting sun streaming in through the windows at the perfect angle. The rise of her arm. The way she stares at me the whole fucking time as she utters the three most excruciating words I've ever heard—excluding the night the doctors announced my parents' deaths. No, this isn't macabre. This isn't death. Quite the contrary, it's a new life together.

It's my worst nightmare.

And it's been coming for years.

"We're getting married."

My eyes fall to her fourth finger where an elegant diamond ring decorates her hand. I smile like a fucking robot, saying the word everyone is expecting me to say.

"Congratulations."

I take the glass of bubbly my brother offers me and I even take a sip as everyone makes a toast of well-wishes. I know all of this is happening. I can hear, somewhere in the distance, the celebration just feet away from me. I nod, I hear, I cross my arms tighter to my chest because, *inside*, I'm dying.

My heart, which had only just begun healing from all those years ago, shatters once more. I think I hear it fall between my rib cage and drop to my other organs.

They're shutting down too. One by one. But before I fall to the floor and make a complete fool of myself, I slip away from the gathering and lock myself in the bathroom where I proceed to throw up all the contents of my stomach.

It's the second time I've vomited in the last twenty-hours. Unlike the night before, this is definitely an emergency, but I have no number to call for someone to come and save me.

To be Continued in *The Kinky One*

https://geni.us/TheKinkyOne

# The Blonde One

Co-writing this book has been an awesome experience. And I'm so excited we're continuing with the series. We've got some big plans!

Thank you so much for taking the time to purchase our book, we've put our all into it and can't wait to hear which team you're on!

We've kept our identities secret. There are literally four people who are in the know... and we're two of them! This means your reviews and recommendations are super important to us. It also means those two people in the know are pretty awesome, they've been amazing and continue to be beautiful people <3

If you can't tell, I'm super proud of our smutty, smutty minds. *wink*

So I hope you had fun and enjoyed reading this as much as we enjoyed writing it.

# THE BRUNETTE ONE

Woowhee! Co-writing makes everything easier! The plotting gets more twisted, the characters more intense and endearing, not to mention you've got someone holding you accountable. I love it! And little miss Blondie is the best writing partner an author could dream of having. This series is an escape from our normal writing styles. We wanted to venture out into something different, but mostly we wanted to break some rules. Will there be a happily ever after? Yes. We just don't know who it is, yet. Thank you for taking a chance on us and I hope you loved our beautiful River as much as we did.

Also Kai. And Nathaniel. And yummy Tyler.

Because this is a serial-type series, you'll be getting a new book every other month, so waiting won't be too long.

See ya next time!

# Books by N.O. One

**Dark Romance**

**The Escort Series (MF)**

The Rich One ~ https://geni.us/TheRichOne

The Kinky One ~ https://geni.us/TheKinkyOne

The Filthy One ~ https://geni.us/TheFithyOne

The Broken One ~ https://geni.us/TheBrokenOne

The Almost One ~ https://geni.us/TheAlmostOne

The Forever One ~ https://geni.us/TheForeverOne

**KOK (RH)**

Kings of Kink ~ https://geni.us/KingsOfKink

If you'd love to get in touch or find out more about our books, please feel free to stalk us in all the places and join our newsletter.

Here is our linktree: https://linktr.ee/n.o.one

# BOOKS WE THINK YOU SHOULD READ:

# BY MOLLY SHELBY

## Dark Romance

Date with the Devil (MF) ~ https://geni.us/DWTD

# BY EVA LENOIR

Eva LeNoir
Fun Flirty Romance

## Contemporary

### The UCC SAGA

Disheveled ~ http://amzn.to/2arpbXp

Disarmed ~ http://amzn.to/2myvxNn

Discarded ~ https://amzn.to/2vWTRPf

UCC Boxset ~ https://amzn.to/3ljvepE

## Contemporary Standalone

The Wish ~https://amzn.to/2FTiKQB

## Rom/Com

### The Woolf Family Series

Screwed ~ https://geni.us/Screwed

Screwed Up ~ https://bit.ly/3IbfWKb
Screwed Over (coming soon)

# Supernatural

## Soul Guardians Series

Reprise ~ https://bit.ly/3cT9nPe

# BY LILY WILDHART

## Dark Romance

### The Saints of Serenity Falls series (RH)

(You will find crossovers from The Escort series by N.O.
One in the Serenity Falls series by Lily Wildhart, and vice
versa!)

A Burn So Deep ~ https://geni.us/burnaltcover

A Revenge So Sweet ~ https://geni.us/revengealtcover

A Taste Of Forever ~ https://geni.us/tastealtcover

Printed in Great Britain
by Amazon